To Vi

MW00412223

# IF...

"Thanks for making me part of your Christmas Eve celebration!" Love, Kay

A Novel

by

Catherine K. Allen

Catherine K. Allen

IF…

First edition printed December 2015

10 9 8 7 6 5 4 3 2 1

Cover design: Geoffrey S. Allen

Printed in the United States of America

ISBN-10: 1519474911
ISBN-13: 978-1519474919

# DEDICATION

This book is dedicated to my family. Without them, it would never have been written.

To my daughter, Cathie, there is no way I can thank you enough for your encouragement to keep going, for your many trips to wrestle with my temperamental computer, and for setting aside time to read chapters of "IF..." when I needed assurance that I was on the right path.

To my son, Wynn, you deserve so many thanks for your continued support on this journey to complete my first novel. Hours in your den helped me with syntax and revision techniques – I needed that help. And, I must not underestimate the value of your personal library as I searched for answers.

To my daughter-in-law, Diane, thanks for the unending lists of titles to choose from and hitting the jackpot, "IF..."

Covers are so important and how lucky I was when my grandson, Geoff, asked if he might design it -- thanks Geoff for the great job!!

Love has never been a question of age.

I shall never be so old as to

Forget what love is.

From *The Collected Stories of Colette*

By Robert Phelps, Ed.

## 1964

This was the last night of the cruise. Ten days aboard the cruise ship *Noble*, sailing the Caribbean, couldn't end without one last celebration. The party was on.

For Kathleen O'Connell and Kevin Johnson, a new relationship had begun during those ten days. One that held so much promise for both of them tonight was to be special. They were not interested in the casino or a Broadway show – rather the quiet lounge where they had spent their first night together. However, the quiet lounge did not materialize. Soon the room filled with fellow passengers eager as well to make the night one would never forget. Kathleen and Kevin's quiet hideaway had now lost its appeal. After a brief visit with a couple at the next table, they left. No question, they knew where they were headed.

It was a beautiful Caribbean night. Out to the promenade deck, the cool sea breezes were gently blowing and the moon lighted a path for them as they moved on to a quiet spot at the bow of the ship. Time meant nothing to them until the first light of dawn broke, peeking above the horizon and they knew that the ship would be back in port in New York in a few hours.

Their day had been full, and preparing to leave the ship was the last thing on their minds. They had no alternative now but to prepare for the arrival. Hand-in-hand, they took their last walk along the deck, heading back inside. Before leaving Kathleen at her cabin door, Kevin suggested that they meet one more time on deck, early the next morning at their "special place."

Back in his cabin Kevin called cruise services for an early wake up, giving him time to pack and be at the promenade deck to meet Kathleen. He turned in, hoping he would get a few hours of sleep. He couldn't. Sleep was not on his mind – Kathleen was!

Suddenly, there was a loud knock on his door. Kevin was surprised when he pulled open the door to see that it was not she, but a wide-eyed steward standing there. "Sir. You have a message from our communication center. It's an emergency." He handed Kevin the communiqué.

Mr. Johnson. Daughter in car
accident. Now in Parkland Memorial
Hospital. Critical condition. Advise
you return as soon as possible. Her
mother en route. -- Texas Highway
Patrol

Kevin just stared at the steward. "Oh, my God, my daughter's in the hospital. How do I get off? It's the middle of the night." He could feel his heart pounding.

The steward looked at his watch. "It is a little before four, sir. We have already docked in New York. We can arrange to get you off the ship in about ten or fifteen minutes. Customs has been notified. How may I assist you?"

"Hell, yeah, I want to get off. I'll be ready in five."

"Very good. I will..."

Kevin slammed the door, took two steps away, re-opened it, and called down the passageway, "Sorry. Didn't mean to slam the door on you."

The Steward turned, waved, and said, "No problem, sir."

Kevin grabbed the first pair of pants and shirt he saw. Slipped on his loafers, sockless. Threw his suitcase on the bed, tossed in other clothes and shaving kit, then shut it. He started toward the door, but stopped short. *Kathleen! What do I do about her?* He looked around the room. *Can't call her at four in the morning,* he thought. *Uh…A note. I have to let her know.* Frustrated he couldn't tell her, he sat down and quickly wrote her the news, folded the note, stuffed it in a Kingsley Cruise Line envelope, and wrote her name and stateroom number on it.

The Steward knocked again. "Are you ready, sir?"

"Yes. Please take this envelope to this person's Stateroom as soon as I leave. I don't have time, and it's very important"

The steward put the note in his inside jacket pocket, picked up Kevin's bag, and led him to the freight elevator. "I'm afraid you will need to leave through our freight area, sir. If we put down the gangway as soon as we dock, an early riser will think he can leave now. You understand."

"Thank you for all you've done." Kevin shook hands with the steward, gave him twenty dollars, and ran with his suitcase to the taxi stand. "La Guardia Airport. I've got an emergency."

IF...

***

$\mathcal{K}$athleen O'Connell checked her watch. 7:30 am. "Oh, oh I'd better get out of here," she murmered as she left her stateroom, remembering Kevin had said, "*don't be late. Only a few minutes to be alone before we have to leave the ship and suffer the noise of New York*"

In a hurry and anxious to meet him, she slung her purse over her shoulder and pushed her suitcase to the passageway. Many had already placed their luggage to be picked up and delivered ashore to the New York City Customs area.

As her door closed behind her, she noticed an envelope peeking out from beneath it. Not wanting to take the time to read it now, she slipped it in her jacket pocket.

Kathleen arrived at the elevator just as the last sliver of light disappeared before closing. "Wait. Wait. Wait." She paced back and forth in front of the elevator door. "Always when I'm in a hurry. I've got to get up there." Finally, it returned and she reluctantly joined five other passengers. As the door closed, she reached to push the Promenade Deck button, only then to realize the others were going two floors lower. She leaned against the elevator wall, furious she hadn't taken the stairs.

When at last alone in the dawdling elevator moving slowly upward, she thought about last night when they were walking on the moonlit deck. Kevin

was holding her hand, saying, *"It's not over, Kathleen. Tomorrow it's just you and me. Let's meet out here for a few minutes in the morning before we go down to customs."*

The elevator leisurely arrived at her floor, the doors taking their time opening. When the door slid back, she bolted out, running to the deck. The deck was empty. *Well*, she thought, *here I am, but where are you?* She tried to be patient, but wanted to see him.

Kathleen walked up and down the deck several times. As her patience grew thin, her anxiety grew greater. She looked at her watch again. *Five minutes. He's never late. I wonder if I misunderstood.* After holding off five minutes more, she went back to her stateroom -- *maybe he called or left a message.*

She checked the phone. No calls. No messages. She called his room. No answer. "I guess the only thing I can do is stay right here. He's bound to show up," Kathleen said to herself. She sat on her bed while kicking off her shoes, then eased back on a pillow and rolled to one side to relax. There was a crackling sound. *What? Oh...that envelope. Now what could this be?*

Slowly, Kathleen sat up and opened it, believing it was a final accounting from the cruise line. She was surprised to find a hand-written note on the ship's stationary, and read:

6

Kathleen. It's 4 am. I don't want to wake you. A few minutes ago a steward brought me a cable from the Texas Highway Patrol. Don't know how they knew I was on here. My daughter has been hit by a car and is in the hospital. Don't know how badly she is hurt and I have to get to her quickly. She was my first thought but the next was of you. Leave your phone number with the purser. I'll call the ship then call you later. I won't be at my house. Don't know where I'll be. I made arrangements to get off the ship. I love you so much, Kathleen, and never dreamed that things would not go as we had planned. Remember, I love you – and it's not over Kathleen. Forever, Kevin

"Oh, my God," she shouted out loud. Kathleen shoved her shoes back on and headed for the door, though she wasn't sure she knew exactly where she was heading. Tears welled up in her eyes. Her throat tightened.

*Why did he have to leave? Why didn't he just call me? Let me know. It just doesn't make any sense at all. This isn't the thoughtful Kevin I know.*

She rushed to Kevin's stateroom still hoping to catch him. His door was wide open. Looking inside, she could see a room steward making the bed. She asked him excitedly, "Excuse me. Have you seen Mr. Johnson?"

The steward turned, suddenly. "I don't think he is on board, miss. When I received the list of departing passengers, it said that I was free to attend to his room early. Sorry."

Abruptly, Kathleen turned away. *The steward's reading something into that message. That's not true,* she worried and her mind was wandering. *The room steward wouldn't know whether he was aboard or not,* she rationalized and hurried to the chief purser's office.

"No one here? That's not possible." Bewildered, she pounded the counter. She was beyond patience. She was frantic now.

Just then, a clerk came out from the office behind the counter.

"At last," Kathleen said, "can you give me some information, or better yet, let me talk to the chief purser." *Very soon the ship will be completely empty.* She had to do something.

The clerk had heard that kind of angry voice before. It was not always fun and good times covering this desk. "Good morning." Her voice was pleasant.

Kathleen ignored the greeting and said, "Please tell the purser that I'm here about a message that Kevin Johnson had left with him early this morning."

Determined not to arouse this passenger anymore than necessary, she said. "I only wish I could help you, but unfortunately, the purser is not here. Taking care of the debarkation is one of his duties and he is somewhere on the ship doing that. But, I can't say where."

8

"Are you telling me that you're in charge?"

"I'm afraid that's so at the moment." The clerk's phone rang. "Whoops, a phone call. Excuse me." She turned her back to Kathleen and spoke quietly into the phone.

Kathleen rolled her eyes. *I can't believe it. Minutes are ticking away. I'm not getting any satisfaction here.*

The girl at the desk was free again. "Now let's see if I can take care of whatever you need. I can see that you're upset."

"Kevin Johnson in cabin 122 spoke to the purser early this morning," Kathleen said emphatically. "I had a note from Mr. Johnson saying that I was to give some information to the chief purser."

While she was talking, the clerk pulled out a pad and said, "If you will write down anything that might have to do with Mr. Johnson's conversation with the purser, I will see that he gets your message."

*I surely hope so*, Kathleen thought, jotting down her name, address, phone number for Kevin to call, and a brief message.

She left and hurried to the closest deck. *Maybe I can see him leaving the ship.* Less than gently, she pushed through groups of people at the deck's railing waving to those waiting on shore. There were so many on the dock -- but no Kevin. Kathleen wiped away tears as she dragged herself back to her cabin. *Last night we had exactly known our future -- and now there was nothing.*

9

\*\*\*

*M*eanwhile, Kevin rushed into the airline terminal and up to the American Airline's counter. "I need a flight to Dallas as soon as possible. My daughter has been in a car accident and I have to get her right away."

"I'm sorry, sir, about your daughter. Let's see what flights we have available," she said as she looked over the airline's schedule. "Let's see. We have a plane leaving in two hours for the Dallas/Fort Worth Airport."

"I'll take it."

"I need to see if there are any seats available first." Without looking up, she continued to search. "Yes. I have three seats on that flight."

"I just need one. How much?" he asked as he took out his American Express credit card.

Kevin's flight to Dallas left on time and arrived only ten minutes late. He was lucky. There was a taxi right in front of the airport door that wasted no time in taking him the hospital. Once there, the receptionist quickly gave him the number of his daughter's room. He headed for the elevators and just as he got to them an elevator's door opened.

There was no one at the nurse's station, so he quickly walked down the corridor. Kevin finally found her room, looked in. He had not expected to see her sitting up in bed and smiling.

"Surprise!" he said. "How are you doing, honey?"

She reached out and grabbed him round the neck as he leaned down to kiss her.

"I'm so glad you're here," she said, squeezing him hard.

He whispered, "Me, too," as he looked down at her cast and gave her arm a squeeze.

"Daddy!" she giggled. "I broke my ankle and Mommy said I'll have a cast for a month."

"That'll be special at school. Everyone will want to sign the cast."

They talked mostly about school and the cruise from which he just returned. After half an hour he told her he needed to make an important phone call to his travel agent. "I'll be back as soon as possible. I'm just going down the hall. Think of a good game we can play."

As Kevin was leaving her room to make his call, a nurse entered. "Oh, Mr. Johnson. I'm sure you daughter is glad you're also here. Your wife left about five minutes ago."

"My ex," he corrected. "I'm glad to see my daughter is getting good care."

"She's wonderful and will be up and running soon."

11

The travel agent told Kevin he would not be able to call the ship directly, but they offered him the corporate number for the Kingsley Cruise Line in New York. He called the number and was told personal calls to crew are not taken while in port and to call back in a couple of days.

He hung up and said out loud, "Now what do I do?" just as a nurse walked by. She shrugged her shoulders and continued on.

He returned a call to the Kingsley office three days later and learned that they were unable to find any communication for him on the ship. Over the next two weeks he spent most of his time with his daughter who had managed her skills with her crutches and was back in school.

The rest of the time Kevin spent wondering how he could find Kathleen. He had told her he was scheduled to go into the navy two weeks after the cruise ended. Two months later he was sailing the waters of Vietnam.

\*\*\*

Kathleen spent the greater part of the next year searching Texas phonebooks – she never found the right Kevin Johnson.

Kevin spent the greater part of the next year frustrated -- he never found Kathleen O'Connell.

## Kingsley Cruise Line

Fifth Avenue * New York

(420) 555-2145

Dear Mrs. O'Connell:                                    April 3, 2014

The Kingsley Cruise Line Corporation is celebrating its fiftieth anniversary this year. We were so pleased to discover that you were a passenger on our first cruise ship, Noble, fifty years ago. We are very happy to be able to invite you to be our guest aboard the inaugural sailing on our newest cruise ship, Noble II.

It would be our privilege to have you join us. The ship will leave New York on May 9 and returns from our Caribbean cruise on May 19. Your ground transportation by limousine will be provided. In addition, your accommodations will be carefully chosen, and the crew is prepared to meet your every need.

We hope that you will accept our invitation. Please call my private line by April 7. We are looking forward to meeting you.

Very sincerely,
**David Penfield**
David Penfield
Vice-President, Operations
Kingsley Cruise Lines
(420) 555-2146 – Private line

# CHAPTER 1

𝒦athleen O'Connell spent most of the night wide-awake. It had been a long, long time since she had felt special. Not only was she excited about the invitation she had received yesterday, but was also thrilled about taking the trip. Since selling her travel agency two years earlier, life had quieted down. *Maybe too much*, she thought as she rested there.

"Come on daylight," she whispered to herself, wanting to get started preparing for the trip. Eventually, the first light of dawn filtered into the room. She pulled up her blanket, snuggled under it, and lay there for a few minutes longer, thinking about that first Noble cruise. *I wonder if anyone else received an invitation? Hmm, fifty years is a long time. Wonder if I would remember anyone? I doubt it.*

Her white Angora cat jumped up on her bed. "Good morning, Mabel." Kathleen gave her nice soft pats while she rolled Mabel over. "Don't get too comfy. We're not laying in bed this morning. There are things to be done. Looks like I'm going on a cruise!"

Moving Mabel aside, Kathleen slipped into her robe and slippers grabbed her cell phone and the invitation, hurried downstairs, and made a cup of coffee. With the hot drink in her hand, she moved into the living room. The early morning light reached across the beamed ceiling. *I love this room, especially at this time of day. It's so cozy,* she thought as she relaxed in her favorite wingback chair, thinking about all she had to do. A half hour later she was on the go, searching the end table drawer for a pencil and paper.

*If I'm going to take the cruise, I'd better get started.* She jotted down things to do -- buy cruise clothes, call to accept the cruise, pick up my passport from safe deposit box, cancel appointments, stop the mail, ask Amy to take care of Mabel. She finished the list and then called her sister.

"Hi, Lexi," Kathleen glanced at the clock. "Oops, I hope I didn't wake you. I just looked at the clock and see it is only seven."

"It's okay. Your timing is fine. I just got back from walking the dogs. No sign of spring yet. I almost froze out there. But, you're retired. What got you up so early?" Lexi asked.

"It was one of those nights. I couldn't sleep. Are you free tomorrow for lunch? I have a few things to talk to you about."

"I'm free. Lets do it. But what's the mystery?"

"I wouldn't call it a mystery, but I'll tell you everything when I see you. How's noon, if that's okay with you? What about a sandwich at the Corner Cupboard? It's close."

"I'm really curious. I'll be there," Lexi said.

"Great! I have a busy day. Can't talk more now. See you tomorrow."

Kathleen hung up and heard Mabel meowing in the kitchen. "Okay, I'm coming. Your breakfast is on its way." Feeling peppier than usual, she filled Mabel's bowl and poured herself another cup of coffee, then walked slowly up the stairs. The carpeting on the steps had been replaced recently and she wasn't anxious to spill anything on it.

First on her list were clothes. After going through her closet, it didn't take her long to realize she had more shopping to do.

Kathleen looked at her clock. Nearly noon. *I better call the cruise line next and accept their invitation. Don't want to lose this chance. Sure I won't see it again,* she thought as she sat on her bed and quickly dialed the number.

She was cheerfully greeted. "Good morning. Kingsley Cruise Line. Mr. Penfield's office."

"Good morning. I would like to speak with Mr. Penfield, please. My name is Kathleen O'Connell. I'm calling about an invitation I received to sail on Noble II next month."

"Oh, yes. I'll put you right through to him."

A deep voice soon answered, also with an upbeat tone. "Hello, Mrs.. O'Connell. This is David Penfield."

"Good morning, Mr. Penfield. I'm calling to accept your great invitation to sail on the new Noble. What a

wonderful surprise that was. I must say, though, that I'm a little curious about how in the world you found me."

"Wonderful to hear that you're going to join us. I'm sure you'll enjoy your time. Our public relations department scoured our archives for those who were our first passengers on our original Noble sailing. They called as many people as they could find," he proudly noted. "We are so pleased that we found you."

Kathleen smiled and said, "You know, your invitation has brought back so many memories."

"I'm sure it did. One of these days I'd enjoy hearing about them. There are not a lot of people that can take us back to cruising 1960's style!"

"I guess that's true. It will be interesting to see how similar or how different the ships are."

They chatted for a while and Mr. Penfield assured her that all of the pertinent information about the cruise would be sent soon. When they finished, Kathleen leaned over, picked up Mabel, and murmured into her soft white fur, "Life's picking up, Mabel -- even if I am playing a different role these days. You know, I think I still have some things in the attic from that cruise."

# CHAPTER 2

*S*he jumped up and threw on an old wool sweater over her nightgown before she went to the attic. It had been a long time since she had been up there. Down the hall she opened the creaky door leading to the attic stairs and was surprised when the single bare light in the ceiling still worked. Shadows spread widely from the discarded furniture, trunks, and boxes that had been there for years.

She looked around and groaned at the task before her. "Oh boy. I forgot what a mess this is. How will I ever find anything?"

At the head of the stairs a large, old, wicker trunk partially blocked her way. *Well, this is as good a place as any to start.*

As she lifted the trunk's lid, she stepped back from the musty odors to catch her breath, and couldn't believe what she saw. "My wedding album! Finally. This is the last place I would have thought to look for it. Thank you, God," she whispered as she picked it up and held it close.

*This should go downstairs to look at later...but I can't wait.* She leaned on the side of the open trunk and tears ran down her cheeks as she turned the pages. She stared at the photos of she and Gordon standing at the alter, remembering her beautiful dress, the reception, her mother and father dancing, and all those other special moments that day. *How did mother and I ever get this all together only a month after graduation?*

18

Finally, she put the wedding album by the top step and turned to dig deeper into the trunk. *Why am I keeping all this stuff -- old grade school and high school papers, diaries, and boxes of old photos?* She hesitated. *Oh, my gosh. I don't believe it. My maroon gym suit.* She laughed out loud. *No way that will fit any more! I wonder if other people are as bad as I am at holding on to things.* The search went on. She pulled out her first evening dress, a blue two-piece bathing suit, and yearbooks from high school and college and set them aside on the floor.

When she reached back in, she was surprised to find Gordon's navy uniform. Slowly, she picked it up. His Lieutenant JG shoulder boards and ribbons had faded over the years, but the uniform remained immaculate. Kathleen ran her hands across the material, remembering how she had dragged herself through those years, trying to face the reality of losing him, and trying to find a purpose in life. The memory of his death only two years after they had married still seemed like yesterday. *Thank goodness for the travel agency. That job proved a Godsend and that cruise changed my life, she thought -- at least for a while.* She sighed and closed the trunk.

Wonder what else is up here? The hunt was on. She edged her way around the would-be treasures, looking into dozens of boxes and shopping bags, but stopped short when her foot hit an old portable radio. A serge of nostalgia struck again.

*What a time that was.* She remembered the excitement when Gordon returned home at last after two long years in the navy. *Oh, the fun we had, trying to make up for lost time. Happiest time of my life -- buying that old radio to take on vacation to the shore. We were noisy, but it surely was fun. Even found that beautiful place to stay.* Kathleen smiled. *What was its name? The large white boarding house. Window boxes filled with the bright red geraniums so pretty as we came up the driveway. What was it called?* She thought for a moment. *Summer Escape. Wow. What made me think of that room we rented? Hard to believe that was over fifty years ago.* Kathleen took a deep breath. *We surely lucked out and were happy. This darn attic is all about us -- all about me -- well, I could get lost reminiscing and that's not why I came up here.*

She slid the radio out of the way with her foot. *When I get back though,* she thought, *I'm coming up here again. It's full of surprises and full of junk!* She slid past old furniture and odds and ends. *Obviously, I'm going to have to have a garage sale.*

She pushed on. Just as she was feeling her way around a large overstuffed chair, she tripped over Mabel who had quietly followed her upstairs and had been doing her own investigating. Kathleen fell against an old wooden table. Trying to catch herself, she knocked over a cardboard box that was on top. It fell to the floor, scattering its contents.

"I knew it! I did save things from the cruise!" She took the next few minutes gathering up dozens of boarding passes, plane and cruise ticket receipts, a handful of luggage tags, and menus from around the world collected over fifty years. The last thing in the box was her college blanket folded around a commemorative plate from the first Noble cruise. As she removed it, she looked down to be sure she hadn't missed anything. She noticed a folded, yellowed note stuck in the bottom on top of a faded creased photo.

*Oh my God! Is that…? And could that be that note?*

# CHAPTER 3

Kathleen found a large shopping bag of old clothes nearby and emptied it on the old, dusty table she had bumped into. She then scooped the memorabilia she had found into the bag. Leaving the attic behind, she hurried down to her bedroom and dumped everything on her bed.

She searched frantically through the bag's contents. As Kathleen continued through the various menus to find the note, the photo fell to the mattress, landing face down. She nervously turned it over. *Kevin!* She stood still with his photo in her hand and stared at it for a minute. *It's him. I remember. This picture was taken when he arrived on board. I was so excited when he gave it to me.* She leaned it up against her lamp as she continued going through the other items.

Under several menus from her cruises, she found the Norwegian Cruise Line menu. As she picked it up, the note slipped out. It was hard for her to believe after all these years it might be his note. She sat on the edge of her bed and glanced at Kevin's photo again. Her hands trembled. Kathleen carefully opened the wrinkled note. There it was. The words he had written to her so long ago.

> Kathleen. It's 4 am. I don't want to wake you. A few minutes ago a steward brought me a cable

from the Texas Highway Patrol. Don't know how they knew I was on here. My daughter has been hit by a car and is in the hospital. Don't know how badly she is hurt and I have to get to her quickly. She was my first thought but the next was of you. Leave your phone number with the purser. I'll call the ship then call you later. I won't be at my house. Don't know where I'll be. I made arrangements to get off the ship. I love you so much, Kathleen, and never dreamed that things would not go as we had planned. Remember, I love you – and it's not over Kathleen. Forever, Kevin

She sat there, stunned. Now, fifty years later, Kathleen's heart beat faster just as it had when she read the note the first time. She often wondered if he really tried to get in touch, or even if he had a daughter, and if she had an accident. *Could he have used his daughter's accident as an excuse to say goodbye - forever? Oh, God.* Kathleen hoped not. She wondered, too, if he ever thought of her. These were questions she had no answers to and probably never would.

*I have been pretty content with my life,* she thought. *Do I really want to bring up a romance that we had fifty years ago and lasted only ten days? Suppose they found him and he's on the cruise, too? Damn, though, that would answer a lot of questions. I don't know what to do! You'd think I was sixteen, not seventy-five. Get a grip, Kathleen. It's been fifty years. Why do I care if he's there?*

She grabbed her phone and called her sister. "Lexi, how about lunch today instead of tomorrow. I really need to talk to you."

"Sure, but you sound strange. Why don't I come over and..."

"No," Kathleen interrupted. "I need to get out of here. See you in an hour."

"That's fine, but I can be at your place in ten minutes," Lexi argued.

"Nope. See you at two at the Cozy Corner." Kathleen hung up.

When she arrived at the restaurant, Lexi was sitting at a table by a window. "Hi. Is this table all right?" Lexi asked.

"It's fine."

"You didn't sound like yourself on the phone. What's wrong?" Her sister's look turned serious. The waiter took their order and Lexi, anxious to know what was going on asked, "Alright, now what's on your mind?"

"Well, an unusual thing happened yesterday and I want to run it by you. Honestly, Lex, it's been a roller coaster morning. In yesterday's mail I received an invitation. A cruise line I was on fifty years ago wrote and asked if I would be their guest on their new ship."

"Wow, lucky you!" Lexi said a little louder than she had intended. Several people turned and looked toward their table. "You travel agents do get all the perks."

"Not since I sold the agency and retired. The Kingsley Cruise Line apparently searched for people who had sailed on their first ship, the *Noble,* fifty years ago. Good for advertising, I image. My name came up. I've been invited to sail on their new ship leaving on May 9th, but I've been thinking about it. To go or not to go is the question."

Lexi leaned across the table toward her sister and spoke quietly this time. "You haven't been on a cruise for years. Why wouldn't you go?"

Her sister took a moment to think, her eyes downward.

"Kathleen?" Lexi hesitated, and then raised her voice. "Kathleen! I have all afternoon and I'm your sister. It's okay, let's talk."

"Sorry," she said and looked back to Lexi. "Well, I was really excited when the invitation came. I even went up to the attic this morning looking for some memorabilia from my first cruise. You know how I keep travel information." Kathleen leaned forward in her chair. "Oh, but before I tell you the rest of the story, guess what I found -- my old gym suit."

Lexi howled, again drawing looks. "Did it fit?"

"Nope." Kathleen responded quickly, having other things on her mind. "While I was looking around up there, I found more than I bargained for -- letters from Gordon while he was in the service, his uniform, and pictures of our wedding. Several of Mom and Dad. You'll want to see those."

"Your right," Lexi said, smiling. "We don't have very many pictures of them. Be sure to save them."

"I will, but what you haven't heard is that I found a note from someone." Kathleen began to play with her napkin. "I met him on that first *Noble* cruise and he could turn up on this one."

Lexi sat back, confused. "What? You kept a note for fifty years? And what's so bad about seeing him again?

"I'm not sure I want to go through all of that. What if a conversation might come up? I got him out of my system years ago. Decades," Kathleen told her.

"Just the same, uh, when was it?" Lexi asked. "19… uh, something. Not yesterday."

"1964. True. The whole thing has shaken me up though, Lex. Honestly, I didn't know that I had saved that note." She avoided her sister's eyes for a moment then looked back at her. "His name was Kevin Johnson. You probably don't remember. It was a few years after Gordon died."

"It sounds vaguely familiar."

"Well, he'd written the note to me way back then. I'd forgotten about him years ago, but there was the note this morning -- and he was back." Kathleen nodded and smiled. "I know. I'm a little too old to think about a man I met fifty years ago. Crazy as it may sound, I guess in my subconscious mind I hadn't forgotten him. I honestly thought it was more than a shipboard romance. It took me a long time to realize it wasn't the real thing." To herself she said, *and I'm still not sure if it was or not.*

"Then why did you keep this guy's note?"

Kathleen sighed. "I didn't know I had. I was surprised when I found it in a box in the attic."

"That's interesting, but what's up?"

Kathleen unconsciously ran a finger across the gingham tablecloth. "Well, I'm not sure that taking the cruise is going to be fun now."

"Why not, for crying out loud?"

"I just have a feeling that if I go, I may see him and he may not even remember me."

"Give me the damn ticket. I'll go," Lexi said, trying to lift her sister's spirits. "Kathleen, this is crazy. Think about it. It's a great opportunity. The other situation happened half a century ago."

"Until I got to this age, I didn't realize that long ago doesn't always seem so far away," Kathleen admitted.

"It's time to drop your hurt and focus on today. Tell you what. Let's have lunch and then why don't you come with me. I've got a few things to pick up at Walmart." Kathleen heaved a sigh. "You're probably right. Hope so! Let's go after lunch. I need to buy a few things, too."

When Kathleen returned home, a large manila envelope from the Kingsley Cruise Line was leaning against her front door. Anxious to see what they had sent, she went directly into the kitchen and poured herself a glass of wine, then sat down at the table and went through everything -- tickets, transfers, three leather baggage tags, the cruise itinerary, and an informational guide. It was all there.

She finished her wine, then went into the den and turned on the computer. *Maybe if I get a look at this ship, I'll feel better about going,* she thought. She pulled up the Kingsley Cruise Line website showing the new ship and dozens of pictures -- larger staterooms, balconies, satellite TV, art shows, a beautiful spa, the casino, and a picture of a glittering revue. There were gourmet menus and itineraries. Even, clips of sports available aboard ship. She had to admit that it all looked pretty special.

What really aroused her interest were photos of a golf clinic in action. Playing golf was a sport that Kathleen loved. *Hmm, I hadn't thought of that.* The last photo was a scene from the ship fifty years earlier. In the picture was a waiter serving drinks on deck. She swallowed hard, staring at the screen. *It seems like yesterday. I think that's where I was sitting when I met Kevin.*

Kathleen couldn't believe that these recent events were turning her into this strange uncertain woman. For years she had moved beyond those ten days at sea. She had become a successful businesswoman, well traveled and well liked. The owner of a large travel agency. Now she was unexpectedly caught up by the past -- anxious and uncertain. She abruptly turned off the computer, swiveled around, and looked at Gordon's picture across the room. I know what you'd say – "Have a great time and stop worrying."

Concerned about Kathleen, Lexi called the next day. "Hi, Sis. How are things going?"

"Fine. Glad you called. I received the package with all the information from the cruise line. It's tempting alright. I looked at their website last night. It all looks great."

"They're ready for you, Kath. Get out of that house for a while. Just go and enjoy yourself!"

"You're probably right."

"I am right. Have some fun. When are you going to have another opportunity like this? Life is short -- enjoy it!!"

"Okay. I've made my decision. I'm going."

# CHAPTER 4

The next few weeks were hectic. Kathleen had to adjust some of her scheduled committee work at church, doctor's appointment, arranging for Mabel's care, and to her attorney about her mother's estate. She was rapidly checking off her list.

She finally found time to call her sister. "Lexi, I could use your help shopping for clothes for the cruise. I need a few things. Are you free tomorrow?"

"Yes, but can we go afternoon? I'm getting an estimate for new carpeting in the morning," Lexi asked.

"Sure, how about around two? We could meet over at Bloomingdales in Stamford."

"Perfect. I'll meet you there."

That afternoon, at Bloomingdales, Kathleen threw caution and a good amount of cash to the winds. Walking into the store, she told Lexi, "First I'd like to look for some things I can wear in the evening."

Lexi slid her arm through her sister's. "Well, let's go look."

They stopped at *"Petites."* Kathleen pushed dress after dress along the racks until she found a couple that she liked. One, a simple long black dress, was exactly what she hoped she would find. Standing in front of a three-sided mirror, she asked Lexi, "What do you think?"

"Love it. Good length, and the neckline is perfect for you -- and wear that long strand of pearls of Mom's. Every good-looking black dress needs pearls."

"That's a great idea and I just bought shoes that will go with it."

"Then buy it and the silk print, too,"

Kathleen looked at the price tags hanging on the sleeves. "They're pricy. I wonder if I should just take the black one or both."

"For heavens sake, stop wondering. You are the guest of a major cruise line. You have to look good."

Kathleen smiled, she was right. "After I change, let's go over to '*Casuals*'."

It was not long before she had picked out three lightweight slacks and several pretty tops, some with bright tropical patterns, and a jeweled shell.

"I can't remember the last time I went on a shopping spree like this. On that first *Noble* cruise, the name of the game was bargains! No bargains this time, that's for sure," she admitted as they walked to the register. "Whoops. I almost forgot. I still want to get a sweater and a pair of deck shoes."

"Are you expecting it to be cold in May in the Caribbean?" Lexi teased.

"No, but the evenings get cool on deck and sometimes the air conditioning can make it a little chilly inside."

They walked around several sweater racks before Kathleen chose a long sleeve, light blue, cashmere cardigan.

Lexi touched the sweater. "I love cashmere. It's so soft. Don't forget. You said you wanted to get shoes, too."

"Right, I need deck shoes. I don't have any."

Later, carrying packages of slacks, tops, shoes, and dresses to Kathleen's car, they looked as though they were in the midst of Christmas shopping. Before leaving, Kathleen turned and hugged her sister. "You know what? You're a really good sister. Thanks for getting me moving. I needed a push."

"You're going to have a great trip. Don't worry about things so much. Just relax and enjoy. That other ship has sailed."

Being realistic about it, Kathleen had decided that there was little chance of her finding Kevin after fifty years. It was a miracle that the cruise line had found her. She had to admit she was getting excited. *It's amazing what new clothes can do for a woman and a brand new ship to wear them on wasn't bad either.*

The week before she left, she had her hair and nails done, picked up her dry cleaning, and went to the bank for traveler's checks and her passport.

The day before the cruise she was emptying the refrigerator when Lexi called. "Hi. Just wanted to make a last minute check. Is there anything I can do?"

32

"Nope. I'm in good shape. Just pulling out the last of what's left in the refrigerator. Need any lettuce or tomatoes?"

"I'm fine. Maybe one of your neighbors might like them."

"Good idea. I'll give them to Amy when I take Mabel over."

"Sounds as though you are all set. Now relax, enjoy the moment."

"I will. Thanks again for all your help, Lex. Stay safe while I'm gone."

"I have your return time. I'll be at the pier to pick you up."

"Hey, you forgot. I'm an important person," Kathleen kidded. "My limousine will be waiting to pick me up!"

"Whoops, so sorry!" They laughed and said goodbye.

Kathleen looked out the kitchen window and saw her neighbor's car in the driveway. She grabbed her phone.

"Hi, Amy. Is it a good time to bring Mabel over?"

"Sure, I'll put the coffee on," Amy offered.

"I'm running a little behind. Think I'll have to pass on that, but I'll take a rain check. Be right over with Mabel, though."

Kathleen walked next door with her cat in one arm and a shopping bag of food in the other.

"Wow. Mabel eats a lot!" Amy kidded.

"It's not all for Mabel, she doesn't eat lettuce and tomatoes." Kathleen laughed, letting Mabel jump down. Putting the shopping bag on Amy's counter, she said, "Thought you might be able to use these, though."

"That's great. Now, is there anything you want me to do while you're gone?"

"No. I think I'm all set. I just need to take the trash out in the morning. Then, I'm off."

"You must be dying to get going! Send a postcard, if you get a chance. I promise to read it to Mabel!"

"Good idea. Thanks. Spoil Mabel a little. She'll love it. The postcard is on its way."

Kathleen leaned down and picked up Mabel. She needed to hear that purr one more time before she left. Mabel snuggled for a moment then jumped back to the floor. Kathleen hugged Amy and thanked her one more time then returned home.

It had been a long day. Kathleen was tired and there wasn't anything left to do. She pulled down the shades and dropped down on the couch.

Kathleen looked around the room. *How many times have I thought about selling this house? Moving to an apartment or townhouse. It surely would be easier.* She closed her eyes and thought back. *Our plans to stay here. Raise our children. Maybe even retire together.* She sighed. *But Gordon's heart attack…cancelled all that.*

34

Though not tired, Kathleen got up from the couch and walked upstairs. *Maybe when I come back I'll talk to a real estate agent. I'd better get to bed. It's getting late.*

The last time she looked at her clock it was two-thirty.

# CHAPTER 5

The alarm went off at 6:00 am. She lay in bed for a few minutes, thinking about anything she might have neglected doing. Soon she pushed back the covers, stretched, and sat up on the edge of the bed. It was a little chilly, so she put on her robe then peeked out the window. *Another sunny day. A good start.* Then she announced, "I need a cup of coffee."

She started down the stairs then remembered that she had cleaned out the refrigerator last night. "No milk. Well, no problem, I'll drink it black," she mumbled. For the next few minutes she moved things around in the cupboard, hoping she would find a hidden box of cookies -- *bad breakfast, but they sure would taste good right now.* No cookies, but way in the back of the freezer she saw one lonely bagel she had missed. *How did I miss that? Glad I did. It'll pass for breakfast with a little peanut butter.* She sat at her kitchen table and ate her makeshift meal.

Back upstairs she took a quick shower, stepped out, and pulled a towel around her shoulders. Passing the bathroom mirror, she hesitated at the reflection.

*Life surely is taking its toll. It's amazing what a difference fifty years can make,* she thought. *At least my grey hair is slow coming in, but my figure's a different story!*

"Well," she said to no one, "I don't see exactly what I want to see. Things aren't great, but at this stage I'll change what I can and accept what I can't." With that, she turned out the bathroom light and went into the bedroom.

As she pulled things from her closet, she remembered how, back then, emphasis had been on how you looked and not how you felt. *I guess at seventy-five, I can't get away with heels quite as high or blouses with necks quite as low.* She chose a pair of navy flat heels and a lightweight navy blue suit. A bright red turtleneck completed the outfit. She always liked turtlenecks. Having finished dressing, she looked in the mirror and thought - n*ow that covers a multitude of sins.* She zippered her two suitcases and carried them downstairs, placing them by the front door.

Checking her watch, she saw that she still had a few minutes. *Wonder if there's anything I didn't take care of? Before I go I think I'll check my emails.* She scrolled through a long list of useless advertising, deleting a dozen before she saw one from Lexi. Why would she write this morning?

> Hi Sis. Hope I caught you in time. One more wish to have a wonderful trip. Enjoy every minute. Send postcards. I thought you would be interested in last night's conversation at church. (Hot discussion about the budget! More when your return.) Gladys asked where you were. I told her you're guest of honor on the maiden voyage of a cruise ship, same company you sailed with 50 years ago. She flipped her lid. (She's so hyper.) Naturally, she took over the

```
conversation. She remembers her
father's story that after her
parents divorce in '64, he took a
cruise to the Virgin Islands, she
thinks, and get this...
```

The doorbell rang. Kathleen jumped. "Darn!" She turned toward the door. "Just a minute. Be right there."

Returning back to the computer screen, she rapidly read the end of her sister's email.

```
Gladys says something about his
meeting a woman on the cruise ship
he nearly married. She went on and
on. Isn't that spooky? Same summer
you sailed. Same ocean. Email when
you can. Love, Lexi
```

Kathleen sat still. *Could it be?* she wondered. *Why this, just before I leave? Oh, well.* The doorbell rang again, twice. "Just a minute, please," she called out. Quickly turning back to the computer, she emailed Lexi.

```
Gotta go. Driver here. Must talk
with you. I'll call from the limo.
Find out Gladys' father's name!
Love, Me
```

## CHAPTER 6

*L*ooking through the peephole in her door, Kathleen saw a tall, thin man with Kingsley Cruise Line embroidered on his uniform coat pocket smiling broadly. She opened the door slowly.

He tipped his hat. "Good morning. I hope that I have the correct address. Are you Mrs. O'Connell?"

"I am," Kathleen said. *He knew who he was looking for. That's good. There's so much on the TV about not opening the door unless you knew who it was.*

The driver continued, "I'm Henry. I'm from the Kingsley Cruise Line."

"I'm ready to go!" Kathleen smiled.

"I knew when I got to Connecticut things would be okay, but getting through that New York traffic is another story and I didn't want to be late. I left home earlier than usual. If I'm here a little early, I'm sorry."

"No, you're right on time. When I go through the city, I always allow myself an extra half hour at least."

Just as she was about to leave her house, the phone rang.

"Tough luck whoever you are, I'm not answering. Henry and I have to catch a boat," Kathleen laughed as she locked the door.

Henry smiled and said, "That's telling 'em, ma'am."

The chauffeur helped Kathleen to the limousine and them put the suitcases into the trunk.

Soon they were on the road. Kathleen took her iPhone from her purse to dial Lexi.

"No battery charge? What is going on?" Kathleen groaned.

"Ma'am?"

"My iPhone has no charge. I thought I plugged it in last night."

"Do you have your charger with you? I can charge it right up here," Henry offered.

"I think it's in one of my suitcases. I hope so. Great way to start a vacation."

"You probably have it. If not, maybe you can get one on the boat, or borrow one," he suggested.

"Perhaps."

Kathleen and the chauffeur chatted. The conversation began with the weather; it always begins with the weather.

Continuing the drive south on route 95, through Connecticut, he commented, "This surely isn't like home - more space."

"Do you live in the city?" she asked.

"Well," Henry began, "we live in Brooklyn. We have an apartment in Bay Ridge. It's close to a park to take our little girl to." He was smiling as he went on. "What she really likes to do most though is to go over to Staten Island on the ferry. My wife and I laugh. My little girl calls it 'going on a cruise'."

Kathleen chuckled. "And it is! How old is your daughter?"

"Samantha Ann's three years old and as the proud parent I have to tell you she's cute. She has blue eyes and red hair, and boy, is she full of it."

"I like her name."

"It's a little long, so we call her Sam, except when she is in trouble. Then it's Samantha Ann. Kids sure can keep you on your toes, but I wouldn't change a thing."

"I can believe that. How long have you been working with the cruise line?"

Henry smiled. "I've been with the Kingsley Line almost 15 years."

"Congratulations," Kathleen said.

"Actually, the congratulations go to you on being the very special guest on this cruise. Everyone has heard about you. You're a celebrity."

Kathleen found that a little hard to believe. "I doubt that, but I am excited to be sailing today."

The conversation slowed down as they reached the city. Henry concentrated on getting through the west side traffic, which is always heavy. Horns blew and brakes screeched. Getting over to the docks at this hour was a nightmare, but then New York is always a challenge for a driver.

Sitting quietly in the back seat, Kathleen enjoyed watching what was going on outside. She loved the city.

It was afternoon when they finally got through traffic and made it to pier 90. There were long lines of

41

taxis and cars at the entrance dropping off passengers. Horns blew, trying to move people. Luggage, stacked up on the curb, added to the confusion. Not only *Noble* II was sailing that day. The piers along the Hudson River had several ships scheduled for Saturday departures.

"Well, here we are, Mrs. O'Connell," Henry said as he inched the limousine into a place along the curb.

Kathleen looked at her watch. 2:00 pm. She sat back, rolled down her window, and watched passengers pouring into the arrivals building. It was a little noisy, but it was exciting and she had to admit to herself that she was scanning the crowd in the hope of seeing his face. *And what would I do if I did?* she wondered. *I've got to stop this before it spoils my trip.*

Henry interrupted her thought. "Like I said, I've been with Kingsley line for years, but would you believe, I've never been on a cruise. Not yet anyway." He got out and came around the limousine to open Kathleen's door.

"Thanks so much, Henry. You've been a wonderful chauffeur." Kathleen stepped out, opened her purse, and removed two-twenty-dollar bills. Handing them to him, she said, "Buy Sam something that she would like. She's a lucky girl to have you for her dad."

"I'll do just that, ma'am. Thanks so much. You have wonderful cruise, Mrs. O'Connell," Henry said, tipping his hat. He then dialed his cell phone. "This is Henry. I have arrived with Mrs. O'Connell." He listened. "Yes. That will work. Thank you."

"Henry. Who did you call?" Kathleen asked, having heard her name.

"Our public relations representative. The Kingsley cruise line is having you escorted through the check-in procedures."

Kathleen raised her eyebrows. "Really?"

Henry looked around. "Yep, here he comes now."

As Henry was taking her luggage from the trunk, she noticed a tall man in a dark blue business suit walking toward her.

"Hello, Mrs. O'Connell. I am Michael Tennyson. Welcome to Kingsley Cruise Line's *Noble* II," he said, smiling broadly at her and extending his hand.

She returned his smile. "It's nice to meet you Mr. Tennyson."

"I wanted to personally greet you. We are so happy that we found you in time for you to join us."

"I'm happy you did, too. Were you able to find anyone else that traveled on that first *Noble* cruise?" She held her breath.

"I wish I could say 'yes'. They may have, but if they did, I'm not aware of it. You won the prize, and we are so glad."

"I'm excited to be here." *Only one thing missing*…Kathleen caught herself in mid-thought.

"Henry will see your luggage is taken care of. Now let's go up to get the formalities out of the way." Mr. Tennyson led her along the walkway outside the busy passenger terminal.

Kathleen wondered what to expect next. As she followed him, she looked toward the terminal windows where passengers were queued up. She had been in that line many times.

"You have no idea how much I appreciate this special attention."

"Special attention is reserved for special passengers. On this cruise you are a special guest. Oh, and by the way, you will find your luggage in your suite."

"My suite?" She was flabbergasted at that bit of information. "Really?" She never had sailed on any cruise line on a suite deck.

"Yes, you're in Suite Nine. We wanted to do everything we could to make your cruise pleasant."

"And you certainly are doing it!"

The noise of the traffic faded as they moved on. They walked to a special section at security where she quickly went through the check-in process, then turned to Mr. Tennyson. "Thank you, again, for making this all so easy."

At that moment, a man in a blue polo shirt and tan Bermuda shorts hurried up to them with a camera slung over his shoulder.

"Before I let you go, I want to introduce you to Jim Wright. He is with our public relations department," Tennyson said.

"Hello, Mrs.. O'Connell." He greeted her with a warm smile. "Would you mind if I took your picture? I'd love to add it to the Kingsley Line archives."

Kathleen agreed. "Of course. I'm flattered."

"Mike, why don't you join Mrs. O'Connell for a couple of shots?" When he was satisfied the photos were what he wanted, he turned to Kathleen. "Thanks so much, Mrs. O'Connell. I think you'll like these. I'll see that you get copies." With that, the photographer thanked her again and left.

An attractive young woman in the cruise line uniform moved close. Mr. Tennyson introduced her to Caitlyn, a stewardess, and advised Kathleen, "Caitlyn will take you to your suite from here. I have to get back to my office. Be sure to contact Caitlyn or the purser if you need anything at all."

"I'm sure everything will be great. Thanks again for making my arrival so pleasant."

They shook hands and he hurried off.

Caitlyn smiled, "If you will come with me, Mrs. O'Connell, I'll help getting you settled in your suite." They walked to the elevator. "Mrs. O'Connell, you'll be staying in Suite Nine on the Starlight Deck."

"That will be great." *Wherever that is*, Kathleen thought.

When they reached Suite 9, Caitlyn unlocked the door and held it open. Kathleen saw her dream accommodation. She stood motionless for a moment taking it all in. Through a floor-to-ceiling sliding glass door, she was able to see some of the beautiful and far-reaching New York Harbor.

Kathleen turned back to Caitlyn. "Sorry," Kathleen apologized. "I was lost for a moment just remembering the first *Noble* ship I sailed on many years ago."

"I understand you were on our original ship. You must have many memories."

Kathleen thought to herself, *you don't know the half of it.* "Indeed, I have. Wonderful memories."

Caitlyn stood quietly aside and let Kathleen take it all in. The stewardess didn't want to rush the moment. Feeling enough time had passed, she went on.

"I'll only take a second, but I would like to point out a few things before I leave."

She opened the armoire door and showed Kathleen a large flat screen TV. Below it was a DVD player. "I think you will find it helpful to know that when you turn to channel 15, it will give you information about onboard activities available and a list of the decks and where they can be found. It will also give you weather conditions, cruising speed, and other aspects of this ship." She pointed across the room. "And over there is a small refrigerator and bar set-up with a choice of wines. After the busy day I am sure you had, you might like to just sit back and have a cool drink."

"A great suggestion, I'll do that."

"As you can see you have a computer on your desk and Wi-Fi Internet is available in all suites. There is other information in your desk drawer, but I'm not giving you time to relax before the mandatory boat drill at 4:00. The instructions are on the back of your door and the location is also on your keycard." Caitlyn put the keycard on the nearby desk. "Oh yes, you will find your life preserver and safe in the closet. Your second-seating dinner is at 8:30." With that, Caitlyn opened the door, and smiled broadly. "I know you'll have a wonderful cruise." She then quietly left the suite.

Kathleen looked around the room and thought, *when money is not the issue, you can surely perform miracles.* The mahogany furniture was a perfect choice to set off the richness of the room. On a low table between the soft, blue, barrel chairs was a large arrangement of yellow, red, and white flowers in a cut-glass vase. Looking around the suite, she took time to enjoy the touches of the decorator. A large bowl of fruit took center stage on the desk.

Kathleen was about to take a few grapes from the bowl when she noticed a small white envelope under the desk lamp and removed the card.

> *You are invited to be the guest of Captain Freeman at his table during the Noble II cruise. Please join him at the second seating this evening.*
>                                             *-- Kingsley Cruise Line*

*Wow, no end to the surprises.* She was beginning to feel giddy with all of the attention she was getting and sat down, kicking off her shoes and still holding the invitation. *Amazing. Lexi was right. A cruise of a lifetime. You're a lucky lady, Kathleen.*

She rested for a few minutes before walking to her suitcases and began opening one when she quickly remembered. *Lexi! Got to call her. Hope I packed that charger.* She rifled through her clothes. No charger. She ran her hand around the suitcase pockets. No charger. She opened her cosmetic bag. No charger.

*Damn. I must have left it home. Better call the gift shop. See if they have them. If they don't, I'm in trouble.* "Hi. This is Mrs. O'Connell in Suite Nine on the Starlight Deck. I seem to have lost the charger cord for my iPhone. Do you sell any there?"

"I'm so sorry, Mrs. O'Connell. We have some phone chargers. Please let me check," the clerk said and returned quickly. "It seems we ordered some chargers, but the shipping has been delayed. I believe they will be here, though, before we sail."

"Thank you. I'll check with you later," Kathleen said, disappointed she'd be delayed in calling her sister.

*Great. Now what? I need to get Lexi's answer. I want to know Gladys' dad's name. She walked around the suite, frustrated. How could I have forgotten a simple cord to charge my phone? Okay. Relax.*

Kathleen went to the computer on the desk. *Wonder if they have Internet? Maybe I can get my emails.* She picked up the stateroom accommodations folder and found the Internet instructions and fees page. *$3.50 set up fee? $.75 per minute? Wow! Better use very few words or type fast.* She sat down and sent Lexi a quick note.

> Arrived safely. Excellent suite.
> Any word about Gladys' dad's
> name? Very curious. Outgoing
> email expensive. Love, Kathleen.

That done, she went out to the suite's veranda to wait for the news. The afternoon sun was low and its reflection pooled in the Hudson River. She stood leaning on the railing, watching seagulls riding the waves. They reminded her of skateboard riders she had seen on TV. Soon she tired and moved over to one of the inviting lounge chairs and stretched out. *Mmm, this is the life*, she thought as she lay back -- this has been quite a day.

*Clang! Clang! Clang!*

Relaxation was immediately interrupted when the intercom came on. The voice summoned everyone to a lifeboat drill. Closing the veranda door behind her, she took her life preserver from the walk-in closet, put it on, and went to the area noted on her key.

Starlight Deck passengers from all of the suites had gathered. It always amused Kathleen to see well-dressed people in their bulky orange vests.

"Attention all passengers," one of the crew began. "Thank you for your prompt response. This lifeboat drill mandated by the United States Coast Guard and SOLAS. Each of you will be assigned a lifeboat, if in the unlikely event the ship needs to be evacuated." For the next 10 minutes he instructed on proper life preserver use and other safety issues.

A redheaded woman in a flowered caftan, standing next to Kathleen, tapped her on the shoulder as they completed the drill. "Is this all there is to it?" she asked.

"Yes and we only have to do it once, thank goodness," Kathleen answered, smiling at her.

"Well thank heavens for that," the redhead laughed and moved off.

Kathleen returned to her suite and pulled open the veranda door again to enjoy the spring breeze.

With time on her hands, she unpacked. When her large suitcase was empty, she opened the smaller one with items from her attic -- menus, daily on-board calendars of events, luggage tags, boarding passes, cruise itineraries, and even the ship's commemorative plate. As she looked at the *Noble* memorabilia she had brought, she wondered, *am I crazy to think that people will find these interesting? I'll drop them off at the purser's office. I'm sure they will find something to do with them since they are a bit of Noble history.*

She picked up another plastic bag. It held a few pieces of sea glass, a couple of small shells she remembered picking up with Kevin, and his note and photo. *Wonder if he saved anything? Maybe I shouldn't have brought these,* she thought as she put the plastic bag in the drawer of her bedside table. *I guess I'm still holding on to a dream.*

She looked at her watch. *Good, I've time to rest for while before I have to get ready.* Kathleen pulled back the white duvet covering the king-size bed and laid down, still dressed.

"Nice," she sighed as her head touched the pillow. *A comfy bed always makes for a great cruise. Should have expected it, though. It's a deluxe suite.* Her eyes slowly closed as a soft breeze eased across the room.

Two hours later, the ringing of the suite's doorbell startled her. Kathleen looked at the clock on the low-profiled bureau. *7:00? Can't be.* The doorbell rang again. Still half asleep, she struggled to get off the bed, running her hands through her hair.

"Yes?" she said through the door.

"It's Caitlyn. I have a surprise for you."

Kathleen opened the door. Caitlyn was standing there, holding an iPhone cord.

"Where in the world did you get that?"

"The girls in the gift shop made a note that Suite Nine needed an iPhone charger. The missing shipment had arrived. They know I am your stewardess and they called me."

Kathleen smiled broadly. "Oh, this is great! Thank you so much."

"You're welcome. Remember. Dinner is in about an hour," Caitlyn reminded Kathleen.

"I know. I overslept. And, thank you again."

Nervousness set in as Kathleen closed the door, afraid the captain's dinner might take place without her. Immediately, she plugged in her iPhone, waited a few minutes then dialed Lexi. Her sister's phone rang several times before she heard Lexi's message machine kick in.

"Sorry I missed your call. Please leave your name, number and a brief message. I will call as soon as I can." Then the beep.

"It's me. Tonight may be a game of phone tag, Lexi. My iPhone is working again, but I'm on my way to dinner. Please leave any information about Gladys' father for me on my email. Love you."

Kathleen quickly took her shower and dressed. The black dress complimented her small figure and the long string of pearls completed the picture. She was really happy with what she had decided to wear. At the lighted mirror in the bathroom, she put on her pearl earrings and touched up her makeup. A little spray on her curly grey-blond hair, and she was ready. She put her iPhone, glasses, and card key along with her invitation for dinner in her black silk clutch, and then took one more look in the mirror.

"All set to go," she announced to no one.

# CHAPTER 7

Kathleen noticed as she left her suite that across the hall another couple was leaving theirs. The woman with whom she had spoken at the lifeboat drill walked over to Kathleen and held out her hand.

"Hi there. I'm Tammy Jamison and this is my husband, Michael," the woman said with a strong Texas accent.

"Good evening," her husband smiled. He was a tall man, his hair slightly grey. Good looking, Kathleen thought.

"Good evening. I'm Kathleen O'Connell. Are you on your way to dinner, too?"

"We sure are, hon. It's been a long time since lunch," Tammy laughed. "I hope that the cuisine is as good as the brochure said."

"Our suites are lovely also, aren't they?"

"They surely are and we paid plenty for them," Tammy quipped.

*Quick with her answers*, Kathleen thought. *These two were going to be fun.*

"What table have you been assigned to?" Tammy asked.

"I'm at the captain's table."

"You're kidding," Tammy said, impulsively hugging Kathleen, her bright red chiffon sleeves billowing out.

"Well, that's a relief. Rumor has it that you never know who might be your dining companions on a cruise!"

Kathleen grinned.

Tammy went on. "Some of my friends just came back from a cruise and said they had less than good luck with the people assigned to their table. They were stuck with them for a week."

"That's too bad," Kathleen said. "They should have asked to be moved to another table when that happened. I think it's probably best to do it on the first night before it becomes awkward." *Darn*, she thought, *I sound like a travel agent. Don't want to go there, or I'll be answering questions for the rest of the cruise.*

Tammy turned to her husband as they entered the elevator. "Hmm. I'll have to tell them, but let's eat first." She turned to Kathleen. "Where are you from?"

"I live in Connecticut. How about you folks?"

"Home is in Dallas and we have an apartment in New York with all those Yankees, but, hon, that's where the money is."

They entered the dining room and were greeted by the maître d' who bowed slightly and asked Michael, "Your names please?"

"We're the Jamisons."

"Oh, yes, we have been expecting you. I recognize Mrs. Jamison from her popular television program," the maître d' said with a slight bow. He nodded to Kathleen and said, "I will be with you shortly, madam."

With that, he led the Jamisons through the candle-lit dining room to the captain's table in the center.

Looking at the sparkling crystal and soft candlelight at each table caused Kathleen to pause for a moment, remembering. She looked around and noticed a man sitting alone by a window, his back to her. *Gray hair. Well dressed...No!* She looked away. *I've got to stop this. This isn't before. It's now.*

After introducing the Jamisons to the captain, the maître d' returned to Kathleen. "The Jamisons tell me that you are Mrs. O'Connell."

"Yes, I am."

"I have kept you waiting and I am so sorry. The first nights are always somewhat frantic," he apologized.

"That moment gave me an opportunity to see your lovely new dining room," she told him. *And to remember my first date with Kevin. It was morning. We played a game of Ping-Pong. I won!*

"You are very kind, but now let me show you to the captain's table."

She glanced one more time at the man sitting alone as she followed the Maître d'.

The men at the captain's table rose as Kathleen arrived.

"Greetings, Mrs. O'Connell. I am Captain Freeman. We are so happy that you are accompanying us on our maiden voyage.

"I can't tell you how happy I am to be here," Kathleen said with enthusiasm, noting everyone was smiling at her. The captain introduced her, and then seated her to his right.

"It wasn't easy finding you, but we did. You're making this an exciting cruise."

"Thank you."

He continued, speaking to his guests, "I really look forward to knowing all of you, but from past experience, I think ordering first allows us more visiting time." The headwaiter passed out menus to the guests while at each place the sommelier poured a dry aperitif, Amontillado, which had been chosen earlier by the captain.

The guests studied their menus. Choices were not going to be easy. Everything looked so good -- Mushroom Charlotte, Spiced Shrimp Supreme, Chilled Strawberry Bisque Soup, Curried Apple Soup, and Salmon Medallions. An extensive salad list was offered -- a pristine Viennese Cucumber Salad, Watermelon with Tomato and Feta Cheese, and a classic Caesar Salad. Last, but certainly not least, palate-provoking entrees - Broiled Salmon Filet, Beef Wellington, Coq au Vin, Roasted Long Island Duck.

"Ordinarily," the captain told them, "Two wines are served with dinner. However, tonight we will deviate. It seems tonight's wines are a gift to you all. Early this afternoon, eight bottles of the very finest wines were delivered to the ship. Accompanying them was a note. From whom, we do not know. Directions on the note asked that they be served at the captain's table. The note explained the gift – 'I could not afford these wines fifty years ago. I am glad that I can now. Enjoy them and allow me this moment as a memory of an earlier time. I wish I could be with you.' The note was unsigned," the captain concluded.

No one spoke for a few moments and then there was speculation.

"Who could it be?"

"Why didn't that person join us?"

"Was it distance or illness that prevented the writer from join us -- or was it something else?"

"It may have been one of the other passengers from the very first sailing of the Kingsley Cruise Line's ship, *Noble*," the captain speculated then nodded to the someliere requesting that the wines be served and remaining bottles set aside for their table.

Kathleen could only speculate on who it might have been. Of course, she wanted to think it was Kevin. He certainly could not have afforded such special wines then -- but could he now?

The captain toasted the absent guest, and then asked Kathleen if she had any idea of who it might be. She shook her head and said, "I only wish I did."

Tammy spoke up enthusiastically. "It could be my dad. This is my first cruise and knowing him, I think he might do that. But, who knows?"

There was not a great deal more said about the gift and the captain turned back to his role as host. "It is customary, on our first night at sea to learn a little about each of you." A warm smile spread across his face.

"Please don't be offended by our curiosity, but we are all anxious to know you better."

He turned to his left. "Let's start with the Nesbitts."

Bob Nesbitt quickly spoke softly to his wife. "You tell them Lily. You're better at this sort of thing."

Lily, an attractive middle-aged blond, squeezed her husband's arm. "I don't know about that, but I'll try. It's never easy speaking first. Well, these last two years have been interesting. Bob retired after twenty-five years as legal counsel for LTR. Our plan was then to travel. However, only a week after we visited our travel agent and set the date for our long planned trip, our world fell apart."

Bob smiled at her and winked. "You may have read about it. We won the lottery," she said flatly.

"How much?" Tammy blurted out.

"Three hundred and fifty million dollars," Lily announced.

After a moment of shocked silence, the table let loose with congratulations and applause. Everyone in the dining room turned, wondering what the cheers were all about.

Turning to her husband, Lily said, "It wasn't all that great, was it?"

He shook his head and said, "You can say that again."

Lily went on. "As you might expect, family that we had never heard of came out of the woodwork. Companies bombarded us with ways of spending our

money. The phone calls never stopped. Life became
hectic." She hesitated. "Just think about it. We were in
our mid-fifties and dreaming of slowing down just a little.
Doing what we wanted to do together. At that point
there was no such thing. I could go on and on, but I
won't. The sum and substance of it is that we gave the
money away."

Kathleen was stunned. "Oh, my gosh. Gave it
away?"

"You what?" Michael exclaimed.

Others were too tongue-tied to say anything.

Even the captain looked shocked.

"Well," Lily went on, "if you think winning the
money caused a life change, giving the money away was
worse. No secret there. The press hounded us out of our
minds, and some of the publicity wasn't kind. It couldn't
be kept quiet. After weeks of research and lots of
conversation, our decision was made. We turned our
winnings over to several hospitals with special emphasis
on caring for children with cancer. Our son had cancer
surgery when he was five. We knew the financial and
emotional impact of that!"

Kathleen interrupted. "How is your son now?"

"Thank the Lord," Lily sighed, "he's fine. Happy,
healthy, and the father of three beautiful girls." She
smiled at Bob. "After all of the legal matters were taken
care of, we had to get away. Voila! This cruise"

Tammy, uncharacteristically, said nothing. The
captain, who had been sitting motionless, shifted forward

and raised his glass toward Lily and Bob. Everyone followed his lead, cheering "here, here." Nothing more need be said.

Tammy, finally recovering from the story, finished her wine. "Well, I'll be damned," she said. "Can't say that I'd be so self-sacrificing, but good for you." They all laughed -- a good reprieve.

There was chatter among them, but soon the captain got everyone back on track. "All I can say is we're proud of you."

Entrees were served and individual conversations continued as they ate. The captain smoothly turned conversations back to learning about his guests as he nodded to the couple next to the Nesbitts. "Now we would like to learn something about you both, Mr. and Mrs. Davidson."

The Davidsons were older than the others and added dignity to their table. Mrs. Davidson wore a soft green dress and a gold necklace and earrings. She looked lovely. A white cashmere shawl protected her from the night chill. Her husband, Joseph, was tall and slim with pure white hair and a well-trimmed mustache. His well-cut tux added to the couple's formal and dignified appearance.

Joseph raised his voice to speak. "Florence is hard of hearing and I want her to know what I am saying." He continued, "Our reason for being here has none of the extraordinary self-sacrifice involved that yours has been," he said, nodding to Lily and Bob. "We are celebrating our seventieth wedding anniversary. Over the years we have sailed on Kingsley line ships almost exclusively. We cannot tell you how pleased we are to have been invited to join all of you at the captain's table for this special occasion." He looked at the captain. "This anniversary is important to us and you have added icing to the cake."

The captain nodded and motioned to the sommelier and when all wine glasses had been refilled, he raised his glass again. Everyone followed suit. "To Florence and Joseph, who have lived a love story. One that we are all privileged to be part of on this cruise."

Joseph leaned over and kissed Florence on the cheek and thanked the group.

*So sweet. I can only imagine.* She stopped and wiped a single tear away. Tears were uncharacteristic for Kathleen, but she had been making up for lost time lately.

The dessert menu was presented. This was the moment that everyone threw caution to the wind and made decadent dessert choices. So many temptations -- Russian Tea Room Cheesecake, Mocha éclairs, Grasshopper Pie, Apple Crisp, Crème brûlée, and Tiramisu.

Kathleen's iPhone rang in mid-bite of her Tiramisu. She dropped her fork and dove into her purse, fumbling to turn it off, but not before she saw it was Lexi calling. She looked at the others. "I am so sorry. I thought it was off. Please excuse me." *Now she calls. I can't leave in the middle of dinner.*

The captain was the first to respond. "Don't worry. It happens to everyone."

"That's true. As a matter of fact, I was in a meeting one time..." Michael started.

"Michael!" Tammy interrupted, bumping him with her elbow.

Kathleen smiled at their sympathy, but her thought about Kevin again briefly overtook her. *Timing is everything. Talk about mixed emotions. I hope it's him and I'll see him again and at the same time, I hope it's not him and I won't have that hanging over my head for the next 10 days.*

"Let's move on and hear from the rest of you," Captain Freeman suggested while his guests enjoyed another cordial.

Tammy toyed with her necklace and thought about what she would say. She had an idea that she might be next. She was right. Captain Freeland gave her a big smile and nodded.

She leaned over to Michael. "Want to do the talking?"

"No way," he said, breaking eye contact with his wife.

Tammy smiled, pushed back her sleeves, folded her hands on the table, and began. "Well, here goes nothing."

Everyone sat back and focused on her. The combination of her Lucy-red hair, and colorful outfit drew attention. Michael adjusted his tux jacket and began fingering his wedding ring.

"Michael and I hail from Texas as y'all might tell from our accents. Unfortunately, we're not there as much as we would like to be. We have an apartment in New York on the fifteenth floor. Michael is writing a book and needs to concentrate. In New York you have to be pretty far up to avoid noise. Of course with me around, there is never complete silence," she laughed and the others at the table joined her. "But lucky for him, I travel quite a bit for my TV program."

"Excuse me, Tammy. What do you mean your TV program?" Lily asked excitedly.

"It's really not that special, but it pays the rent."

Everyone laughed.

Tammy continued, "I do documentaries. The station decides what the public will watch and away I go." She hesitated and took a sip of her wine. "It's necessary for me to interview people and to visit spots that will enliven the hour and entertain the viewer, and then come back to New York to produce the finished product."

"And the apartment is less than quiet for awhile," Michael added, rolling his eyes and taking a drink of his wine.

Everyone laughed again.

"Shhh," she said, spanking his forearm and went on. "I've done presidents, business leaders, and artists." Tammy was enjoying herself with a live audience at the table. "Last month I did something a little unusual. I visited a school in New Jersey, Doane Academy, formerly St. Mary's Hall. It was founded in 1837.

Fascinating place. Originally it was a girls' boarding school, now a co-ed day school. Talk about history. Jefferson Davis sent his niece there just before the Civil War..."

Kathleen broke in. "Oh, I saw that program. I knew you looked familiar, but couldn't decide where I had seen you before."

Tammy smiled. "Hope you liked it."

"I liked it so much that my sister and I took a trip down to see the school," Kathleen said. "You're right. Doane Academy is like reading a history book. Fortunately, we arrived on opening day and were there to see the senior class coming down the Delaware River to the school in canoes. Tradition in action again. It was great."

"Exactly! It was one of the rewards of my job." Then, changing the subject, she turned to the captain. "You know, it's hard to believe that this is our first cruise. I guess it is due to too many deadlines." Tammy took a breath then nudged her husband with her elbow. "Now tell them about your book, Michael."

"I guess that means it's my turn. She's a hard one to follow, but here I go. The subject of my book has no bells and whistles, that's for sure."

"Well, go on." Tammy poked his arm, "Tell them what it has."

"It's actually what you might call a scientific essay. Hope your ready for this." Everyone's face turned serious. Michael cleared his throat. "It's about the theory

64

that cow manure produces gases that in turn can be used as methane. If used in the home, it would considerably lower the annual expense of heating," he explained.

Tammy interrupted, "And that's no bull!" She slapped the table, laughing at her own joke.

No one could keep a straight face.

Michael shook his head. Tammy had had the last word again.

When the laughter died down, the captain moved on. "Alright, now it's my turn. I would like to introduce our next guest myself. I invited my son to join us this week." He looked over at the handsome young man and they acknowledged each other. "He is between travel orders and it seemed like the perfect time. Jim, say a word will you please."

Jim smiled. "Dad invited me aboard because it's rare that we get visiting time. I'm in the navy. With the direction that the navy takes me and the direction that the cruise line takes Dad, we don't hit the same port very often. So, I'm glad we have this time. Thanks, Dad."

After a moment's silence at being Jim's father, he was back as ship's captain. "Now, as I said earlier, our guest of honor, Kathleen O'Connell, was not easy to find. The effort was certainly worth the time, though. With *Noble* II beginning her maiden voyage fifty years after the launching of the original *Noble* cruise ship, the Kingsley Cruise Line set out to see if any of those who had sailed with us fifty years earlier could be found. The idea was great, but making it happen was not easy. He looked around the table. Just try to find the friends you had fifty years ago and you will see what we were up against."

Kathleen knew her turn was coming. *I'm not looking forward to this. What will I say?* She wondered.

The captain went on. "Our people checked and rechecked the manifest list. There was exhaustive searching on our computers, Facebook, and other social media. There were those whose names apparently had changed over the years. Marriage will do that."

Everyone smiled.

"Some had age related illnesses and others had passed away. Remember, we were looking back for people who had traveled fifty years ago and not many of them were teenagers. It's hard to believe we found Kathleen. Fortunately for us we did, she was young on that cruise. In your twenties, weren't you?"

Kathleen nodded.

"We got in touch with her and she said 'yes'. Now, Kathleen, it's your turn. Won't you tell us a little about those intermittent fifty years?"

Taking a sip of water before she began, Kathleen started. "I still find it hard to believe I am back on a *Noble* ship, *Noble* two. The cruise on that first *Noble* was not only wonderful, but it was a blessing. The death of my husband just two years after we were married had sent me into a tailspin."

No one said a word.

"My work as a travel agent was the only thing that kept me going. As a matter of fact, I worked for the same agency for many years and eventually bought it. Sailing on that first *Noble* ship, though, was the best thing that ever could have happened to me. It restored my self-confidence and my self-awareness about life. I was ready to move on. So, you can imagine the thrill of being invited back -- fifty years later."

The captain toasted her, raising his wine glass. "And our reward is having you with us tonight."

Everyone agreed and joined the toast to Kathleen. She nodded her thanks. *I hope I said enough.*

Other tables were now emptying as passengers headed for one of the fantastic shows, seeing a new movie, or taking their chances in the casino. Some of the younger passengers stayed up into the early hours dancing to live music or singing at the karaoke bar. Others took in the midnight buffet. There seemed to be no unhappy people on this ship.

She looked at her watch. *Good heavens.*

The Davidsons were tired after their trip to New York and the lovely evening. Joseph smiled, "Thank you for an evening we'll never forget. You young people go on and have a good time. We'll see you at breakfast." With that, they left the dining room, Florence holding her husband's arm as he carefully guided her through the large dining room.

Kathleen turned to the captain. "If I may, I'll excuse myself as well. Thank you for a long and exciting day."

On her way back to her suite, she thought about the grey haired man sitting alone in the dining room who made her feel a little uneasy. She knew that chances of that man being Kevin were slim, but she hoped she'd be able to confirm that.

Back in her room Kathleen quickly turned on her iPhone. She was anxious to listen to Lexi's voice message.

"Hi, Kath. Got your email. I haven't heard back from Gladys yet. I'll email when I do. Hope you're having a ball. Don't forget the postcards. Lexi"

As Kathleen lay in bed that night, memories began to creep in again. *Guess I have to wait for Lexi. Funny how this is important to me after all the years. Kevin was just a vague memory before I found the note. Will we ever meet again?* She wondered if there was any possibility that he might have sent those bottles of wine for dinner or if he might have booked a stateroom. Her last thought as she dozed off, does red hair turn a pure white over the years?

# CHAPTER 8

The weather the next morning was perfect. A cloudless sky and a warming light breeze. Kathleen, Lily, and Tammy had quickly bonded and had made plans for the day. They knew St. Thomas was duty free. With their credit cards secure in their wallets, they left the ship early and headed for the shopping district.

"Would you like to do a little sight seeing first?" Kathleen asked. "Personally, I don't care. It's up to you two. I've been here several times with clients. I thought you might like to see something of the area."

"You're the travel agent," Lily pointed out. "You tell us where to go."

"This won't be the first time someone has told me where to go," quick-witted Tammy chimed in.

"Girls, I am not a travel agent. I was a travel agent. Well, let's see what I remember. There's the famous Bluebeard's Castle, museums, or maybe a sky ride in a Gondola. People seemed to love that."

Kathleen didn't know either of her companions well enough to know what suggestions would appeal to them.

"No museums. I can see them on TV shows anytime," Tammy said.

"Me either," Lily agreed. "This is a holiday. Museums, no! "

They weaved their way along the crowded sidewalks. Two other cruise ships had docked that morning and it seemed as though everyone wanted to shop at the same time. Some men in drab shorts, tennis shoes, and team-sponsored T-shirts sat on benches outside of stores while their wives or girl friends shopped. Others were off playing golf at one of the manicured courses.

"There are a couple of really fun things to do. There's the St. Thomas "Skyride." Best views of the island from 600 or 800 feet high in a gondola. Great views from the top of Paradise Point."

"No, I don't think so. I hate being off the ground. Nothing high for me, but you two could go," Lily suggested.

"We want to spend the day together. Let's skip that," Tammy said.

"I know a wonderful place for adventure and we don't have to walk up hill or get off the ground," Kathleen said. "Now, this is just what I remember. There was a small submarine that..."

Lily interrupted with a quiver in her voice, "A submarine? You want us to go in a submarine? Like an underwater submarine?"

"No, Lily. A flying submarine," Tammy quipped.

Kathleen thought she better describe in more detail. "Actually, yes. It does go underwater, but not too deep. Only a few feet, but what a view of the fish and plant life.

The water is so clear you can see the ocean floor."

Tammy jumped in. "What a kick. Let's go!"

"Alright. I just hope it's safe, that's all," Lily worried.

Kathleen comforted her. "You'll be fine. I'll sit right next to you."

Passing the stores on their way to the sub was not easy for Lily who really wanted to spend the day duty-free shopping.

A few blocks farther, Kathleen stopped and looked around. "Where's the submarine? I don't know, girls. I'm sure this is where it was."

She continued searching, looking up and down the waterfront.

"There's no submarine?" Tammy asked.

"Nope, I don't see it. At least not here. Hold on. Let me ask someone." Kathleen went into the nearest store and quickly returned. "Looks like that Atlantis sub sailed. Lady inside said its been moved to Barbados. Well, that's progress, I guess. Change happens. I didn't keep on top of that one," Kathleen said sheepishly.

Lily had a big smile on her face. "Let's go shopping then."

Kathleen and Tammy followed as Lily made a beeline toward the shops.

"Well, before we go shopping why don't we stop and have a drink," Tammy suggested. "I can tell it's going to be warm today. Alright, Lily?"

"It's fine with me, for a little while."

"If that's what you want to do, I'd like to suggest a place nearby where we can relax before our attack on the stores," Kathleen suggested. "It's just a couple of blocks away, Lily, so after a drink we can quickly make it over to shop. I hope at least I get this right." Kathleen was not happy she had led them on a wild goose chase.

Tammy grabbed Kathleen by the arm. "Times a wastin'. Show us the way."

Ten minutes later they walked up the steps of the Hotel 1829 and Kathleen led them directly into the hotel's bar.

"Thank goodness. It's still here," Kathleen joked. "Let's choose drinks. Trust me. You just sit back and enjoy."

Within minutes three frothy Piña Coladas arrived and they sat back, relaxed, and toasted each other. They all agreed -- the stop was a great idea.

Tammy took a long sip of her drink and asked, "How did you know this place existed, Kathleen? Did you send clients here?"

"Occasionally. Some clients look for a place with atmosphere and great piña colada choices," she laughed then added, "Fortunately, the owners over the years have kept the original Spanish charm by keeping the hand-painted Moroccan tiles, the beautiful Tiffany window, and the old brick walls. And look over there, the original kitchen hearth. The hotel does have atmosphere!"

Lily was taking it all in. "You're right. It's different from the resort hotels. It makes me feel sort of sentimental. I wish Bob was here."

Kathleen understood exactly what Lily was feeling. "The very first time I came here I had exactly the same reaction."

Tammy looked at Kathleen. "That's a strange response."

"Well, travel agents often are asked for special little inns and hotels. Not all travelers need the security of the familiar. This uniqueness is appealing. It's so different from stateside hotels and from the resort's sandy beaches and palm trees. I love both, but this is a little different -- and special."

"I'm curious. Could this little romantic place mean something special to you?" Tammy nudged for more information. "You had no trouble finding it."

"Don't read anything into that. It's been here a long time and everyone knows about it," Kathleen responded, trying to deflect the question. *If only you knew. You're sitting in Kevin's chair and only a few steps to our room.*

Tammy's career was based on learning the unusual about people and places. "I'm not giving up, Kathleen," she pushed. "Have you ever stayed here yourself?"

Kathleen reached for her drink. "As a matter of fact, yes, I have. On the original cruise we had to stay in St.

Thomas for two extra nights for ship repairs of some kind. It was great having more time on the island, and it was so near the shopping and easy to get back to the ship. If we chose to stay on the island, we could." She shifted in her chair. "At our own expense, of course. All we needed to do was to fill out a form saying where we could be contacted."

"Doubt you could do it today with all of the security concerns," Tammy said.

Lily was getting anxious to move on. "Say. Are we going shopping or are we just going to sit and talk? Besides, it's almost eleven o'clock. We still have to shop, have lunch, and get back to the ship."

As they left the hotel and started down the steps to the street, Tammy tripped and grabbed Kathleen's arm.

"Wow, what happened?" Kathleen asked as she held on to her friend.

"Nothing dramatic. It happens once in awhile. Old injury. I'll live."

Lily was relieved that Tammy was alright and seemed to be moving on without a problem. She didn't want her hurting, but she really did want to shop.

"Okay Kathleen, you're off the hook for awhile but eventually you are going to have to tell us about those two days."

Kathleen just laughed and as they walked to Main Street she announced, "Well, here we are. Shoppers' Paradise -- and duty free!"

There were jewelry stores, dress shops, and the alleys, like Palm Passage, that housed special little boutiques. They were quickly in and out of places that sold tourist knick-knacks.

"Hey, look at that." Tammy pointed to a large jewelry store she saw across the street. "Come on, let's go over and look inside."

"Okay, but remember, I'm just looking. I think prices here are going to be higher than my credit card can take," Kathleen warned.

Once inside, they stopped short, impressed with this well lighted, clean, and wide-aisled store. It was as inviting as any up-scale store in New York City.

"This place is great. I'm heading for the bracelets. Wonder if anything is reasonable." Lily was so glad that she could shop at last and she hurried off.

"Okay. I'm going to check out necklaces. Bet there is something I can't live without. You okay if I go searching?" Tammy asked Kathleen.

"Of course, I want to just wander around and I see there are places to sit if I get tired. Take your time and enjoy yourself."

"Now don't run off with a sailor while we're gone! See you later, Kathleen," Tammy laughed and moved down the wide aisle.

Kathleen was happy that her new friends were enjoying themselves and glad to have time to just wander. She had her own searching to do. Unconsciously, she rolled the four bracelets on her arm as she walked. *Where did we stop? One of these counters, I think. It was so long ago. Kevin really wanted to buy me these silver bracelets. I wonder if he would remember that afternoon,* she thought.

Things had changed over the years. It was still the same jewelry store. It had the same name. But now it was a far more modern establishment. Kathleen walked around for a while enjoying it all. There were clusters of comfortable looking chairs placed in various areas around the store. She was happy to see some chairs near a glass case displaying a collection of Swiss watch brands. She spent a little time looking at them though her wristwatch and band were fine. *They're just a little beyond my budget,* she joked to herself then sat down, relaxing and enjoyed the pianist playing. The music floated across the store.

Before long, Lily retraced her steps and found Kathleen. "Here you are. I've been looking for you. Are you tired?"

"No, I'm fine. Just decided to sit back and enjoy the music for a few minutes. Did you find anything?"

"Yes, and I'm so pleased." She took a small white bag from her purse and showed Kathleen a charm bracelet. "It's for my daughter-in-law. She'll love it. I added charms of the children, a dog, and their house. They just bought a new one." She held out the bracelet for Kathleen to see.

"That was a great idea. I have a feeling that you approve of your daughter-in-law."

"You bet I do. Diane and I are very close. I'm so lucky."

Lily stretched out her arm. "And for me, these wonderful sterling silver bracelets. I noticed yours and decided I wanted some, too."

"They really are a lot like mine. Expensive?"

"A little, but worth it," she smiled.

"Have you seen Tammy recently?" Kathleen asked.

"No, I haven't. Let's go and hunt for her."

They caught up to Tammy looking at necklaces. "Oh good, glad you're here. Need your opinion." She held up a chunky yellow and bright green tourmaline necklace. "This one is a knock out, but I'm feeling sort of sentimental about this other one."

Resting on a piece of black velvet was a beautiful silver necklace with an interesting red shell hanging from it. Tammy picked it up gently, swinging the shell back and forth. Kathleen and Lily agreed that it was lovely.

"My dad has a brandy snifter on his bureau at home that is filled with shells he has collected all over the world. I think I'll buy this necklace. It will make him happy I remembered his 'memory shells' as he calls them. He always takes one with him when he travels. 'For good luck,' he tells me."

While they waited at the desk for Tammy's necklace, Lily quietly said to her, "You know what? It's really good to see a little of this side of you. Just got a peek, but I really liked what I saw. That sentimental side that you keep hidden. Am I right?"

"Close enough!" Tammy said without emotion.

Lily joined Kathleen who had walked over to look in another case. "Did you find anything that appeals to you?"

"No," Kathleen replied. "Window shopping is more my speed -- and less expensive."

"You're right about that. Now let's get going. I'm starved and my feet hurt," Lily urged.

"Any connection between the two?" Tammy laughed. "See, Lily. You wanted to go shopping and now you're paying for it!"

They were satisfied with what they had purchased and ready for any suggestions Kathleen might have for lunch. Their tour guide partner thought for a moment. "Maybe. The Inn of the Gods would be a nice choice. It's so pretty up there and it has the world's best daiquiris." Kathleen had taken small groups there many times.

"Well, lets go do a little taste testing." Lily was enjoying it all.

Before leaving the store, they asked a clerk where they could find a taxi. "Taxis love us," he said smiling. "There are always one or two waiting outside. Our clients are never inconvenienced." He looked out the window. "You're in luck. Walter is outside. He doesn't have a traditional taxi, but all our customers think he's great."

Tammy laughed. "Good. A taxi by any other name is still a taxi. Let's go."

They thanked the clerk and walked to the shiny, maroon, four-door Buick that was waiting outside. The driver jumped out of his car.

"Are you Walter?" Tammy asked.

"I am and I'm at your service," the driver said with a big smile, tipping his hat.

"Well, Walter, we would like to go the Inn of the Gods," Kathleen told him.

"A fine choice, madam."

As they drove along in the bright sunlight, they passed the busy harbor filled with sailboats, fishing boats, and big cruise ships anchored along the docks. As the road curved up, they were rewarded by the spectacular views of the island. Finally, they turned down a quiet country lane, lined with lush greenery and colorful flowers. Before them at the end of the lane was the Inn Of The Gods, a picture perfect building -- a white plantation. The surrounding gardens were a mass of bright colors -- lilacs, freesia, hydrangea, larkspur, daisies, and the low fence circling the porch was a mass of pink climbing roses. It was beautiful.

"Your right, Walter, an excellent choice," Lily nodded to Tammy. "Our travel agent did it again."

They were warm and tired and anxious to get inside.

"It was such a pretty ride up here. Now what do we owe you?" Tammy asked.

"Whatever you feel is the right amount ma'am."

"You have no set fee?" Tammy asked

"I don't exactly have a taxi license so I can't take your money by hand. Please put whatever you think is reasonable on the floor."

Tammy thought it strange, but she placed the money under the edge of the floor mat. They thanked the driver and walked up the steps of the inn.

The lobby was large and inviting, cooled by the palm-shaped blades of the ceiling fan. Large colorful Van Gogh prints of "Iris," "Poppy Flowers," and "The Red Vineyard" covered the bright white walls. Beneath the paintings were couches with fabrics chosen to compliment the pictures -- green, lavender and poppy red.

Soft background music filled the lobby. An attractive young hostess greeted them. "Good afternoon, ladies." She smiled and suggested, "you might enjoy it out on the cool veranda. It's a good place to relax and maybe have a drink. If you find you'd like to have lunch with us, just let your waiter know."

"Good idea!" Tammy was all for a comfortable spot and a drink.

They took her advice and moved to the cooling air on the veranda.

"Look at this!" Tammy hurried over to a view of the harbor. "You know, if they only had guest rooms, I might skip the ship and stay here," she told the other two.

"Make it a twin-bedded room," Lily laughed.

They sat down in huge inviting pillow-filled white wicker chairs facing the harbor. Next to each chair was a low glass-topped table with beautiful long-stemmed lilies. Soft breezes cooled them. If they were teenagers they might have wanted things a little livelier -- but they weren't teenagers. All they wanted was a nice comfortable cool spot, and they had it.

Tammy sighed rather loudly. "I don't know about you, but for me it's a drink, lunch, and back to the ship. Time ashore is great -- for a while."

Lily popped off her sandals. "This may not be the thing to do, but I'm doing it anyway. As I said before, my feet are killing me."

"Go for it, Lily," Kathleen encouraged.

"Thank God the veranda has a bamboo roof covering us. I wouldn't like sitting out in this noonday sun without it!" Tammy relaxed against the pillows.

In a short time, a waiter quietly moved toward them. "Good afternoon, ladies. May I get you a drink?"

Tammy wasted no time ordering. "It's a strawberry daiquiri for me. How about you two?"

They both agreed that was a good choice. Kathleen asked that a table be reserved for them for lunch.

"Thank you, ladies," the waiter said, bowed and left. It was not long before he returned and placed their drinks on the glass-topped side tables next to their chairs.

The three quickly picked up their drinks and enjoyed the moment.

Soon Tammy, swirling her drink, was at it again. "I love a little quiet, but not too much. Now its time for girl talk. Hey, I'm curious. Kathleen, you told us you were a widow. But you never told us if you married again."

Believing a simple sentence would quiet Tammy, Kathleen said, "I was not as lucky as you two are." *Tammy is a lot of fun, but she's so curious about everyone and everything. Guess it's part of her job. I wish she didn't push so hard though.*

"Lets hear a little more about you. You're the mystery lady." Tammy winked at Lily.

Kathleen shook her head. "I don't qualify as a mystery lady, that's for sure!"

"I'm not so sure about that," Tammy argued.

"You know I was married right out of college. Big plans for us fell apart. I told you I lost him."

"Never found anyone else in fifty years?" Tammy raised her voice. "Hard to believe."

"To satisfy your curiosity, Tammy, I did meet someone. Wish I had exciting news for you. It didn't work out."

"Details, details, girl friend," Tammy encouraged.

Lily didn't have a lot to say. She just sat forward eager to hear what was coming next. Kathleen was not keen on continuing the conversation about her, but knew that Tammy would not be satisfied unless she said something.

"It's as simple as this. We met on board the first *Noble* during our ten-day cruise. We fell in love. I know,

82

that sounds pretty impossible, but it happened. Because of botched communication in the Purser's Office, he never got my address and phone number and I never got his. It's a long story with no answers, I never saw him again."

Lily, always the comforter, spoke up. "We shouldn't have pried."

Tammy jumped. "Like hell we shouldn't. This could be a made-for-TV movie."

Kathleen remained noncommittal.

"Okay. This calls for another drink before we have lunch." After ordering, Tammy went on. "Kathleen, it's never over as long as you're breathing. Just keep looking around the corner. You never know who might be looking back at you."

Kathleen laughed, "Thanks for the advice. I'll keep checking. Ladies, you'll never know how many corners I have checked. I think I gave you a pretty good thumbnail sketch of me at dinner last night."

It was not long before the waiter returned and placed their second round on the tables and said, "Thank you ladies. A table has been reserved for you for lunch at your leisure."

Kathleen soon rose. "Well girls, let's go see what's on the menu." They followed the waiter to a sunny dining room where Lily suggested that they have a table away from an open window because of the too bright sunlight. Vases filled with fresh lilacs and daffodils were centered on pure white table clothes. The warm

Caribbean breeze softly moved the sheer lilac-colored curtains at every window.

They spent time studying the menu since everything seemed delicious. There were salads, quiches, sandwiches, and interesting specials of the day. They ordered then sat back finishing their drinks.

Kathleen was delighted to see that the conversation had become shopping and the cruise -- not her love life.

"You are so lucky to have sailed on the first *Noble*," Lily said. "And even more lucky that you hung around long enough to do it again. Oh, my gosh, that sounds weird."

They all laughed.

Tammy never let her curiosity waiver. She looked at Kathleen and said, "Now we've ordered, on with the drama!"

Kathleen knew what Tammy wanted. "Well, after my husband died, I buried myself in the travel business. Thank heavens I had it to keep me busy. The agency was offered familiarization trips by cruise lines from time to time. One came across my desk that looked interesting. I checked to see if there was still any available space. One cabin left. I grabbed it. It was the inaugural sailing of the first *Noble* cruise ship."

"When was that?" Tammy asked.

"Back in 1964."

"I think I may be brain dead." Tammy knew immediately it was a stupid question. "We're on the 50th anniversary celebration."

84

"Is it really true that travel agents get great deals?" Lily asked.

Kathleen smiled. "Everyone thinks so and once that was true. Now less often. These days the computer is as important to the cruise companies as the agent. It has become quite common for cruisers to make there own reservations. Well, there's not much more to say other than I stayed with the agency, eventually bought it, and now I'm retired."

She was off the hook, at least for a while. They enjoyed the rest of their lunch. The hostess arranged for a taxi to take them back to the ship.

During the taxi ride, they talked about their evening plans. Tammy had called early in the morning to invite them to join her and Michael for a drink before dinner in their suite.

"Thank you, again, for inviting us tonight," Lily said.

"I thought it would be fun having our spouses mingle with us. You know, find out what they did today. Remember, if they get too involved with their golf game, we'll need to slow them down. Talk about something interesting…like shopping!"

Kathleen's iPhone rang. Searching quickly, she opened her purse and took out her phone, and saw the text was from Lexi.

```
Bad news. Wrong ship. Wrong man.
Sorry. Where's the postcard? LU,
Lex.
```

"Sorry to interrupt the conversation. It was my sister sending me a message from one of our church ladies."

"Well, it couldn't have been bad news," Tammy inquired. "Looks like it was a short message."

*She's still checking me out*, Kathleen thought as she put the phone away without comment.

Tammy went on, "I thought it might be nice to get together for a little while," she told them. "Farewell to St. Thomas is the theme. I invited Florence and Joseph. I think they were pleased to be included. Sorry to say, though, that the captain and Jim had other plans. Jim's girlfriend, Abby, is on the ship and the three of them have a previous invitation this evening."

Kathleen spoke up. "I met Abby this morning when she and Jim were going ashore. What a good-looking girl…"

Tammy interrupted. "Lucky Abby. Not a bad looking escort, either. As for the others, I know our golf buddies are going to be exhausted. Getting together for an hour or so will give them time to lay back, have a drink, and visit a little before dinner.

# CHAPTER 9

Everyone arrived at the Jamieson's suite dressed for the special dinner that was to honor the inaugural sailing of the first *Noble* ship. It was a formal evening and they all looked forward to it.

Joseph and Florence were first to arrive and greeted by Tammy. "Welcome. Florence, that is an exquisite lace gown. I love lavender. You look lovely."

"It's a present from Joseph for our anniversary cruise. Our daughter took him shopping. I love it, too." Florence reached for Joseph's hand.

Michael jumped in. "Joseph. You're a knockout tonight, too," he said, kidding. "You're tuxedo is smashing."

They laughed as Kathleen, Lily, and Bob arrived at Tammy and Michael's door together.

Tammy hugged each of them. "Great. The gang's all here." She took Kathleen's hands. "You look so fashionable and I promise, no questions tonight. You'll surely stand out as the special guest."

Kathleen was pleased with the word *fashionable*. When she purchased the dress, the sales woman had called the dress an "eye catcher." That had concerned her a bit at the time, but she loved it and bought it. "That's nice to hear, Tammy. When you wear something that you have had in the back of the closet for a couple of years, you wonder if it is still in style."

Tammy raised an eyebrow and said, "Oh sure, a couple of years -- not."

Michael, standing at the door with Tammy, tapped Kathleen on her shoulder. "I noticed that you are wearing a lovely pin on your dress this evening. Any special story about it?"

*Oh boy*, Kathleen thought. *Looks like curiosity runs in the family.* Kathleen touched the pin. "No, but thank you for asking. I've had it for years. A friend gave it to me a long time ago." *Why did I say that? Good Lord, I had completely forgotten about how I got it.*

To change the subject, she said, "And Michael, aren't you the dapper one."

"Well, thank you, Kathleen. That, madam, deserves a drink."

"A little red wine would be nice."

With a gleam in his eyes, Michael turned to Lily and Bob. "May I get you a bottle of wine?"

"That might be a bit much for tonight," Bob laughed and turned to his wife. "Lily, can Michael talk you into a special label from his wine cellar?"

"Lovely, dear. Maybe I can enjoy it at home while I'm reading Michael's book and thinking of how many cows we'll need to lower our electric bill."

The three of them laughed. Everyone was in top form.

Tammy walked up to Lily. "Did Michael pull his old joke about having a bottle of wine? He really thinks he's funny. More importantly, though, I love your elegant dress."

"Thank you. It's not new. Bob likes it's so much, I decided to bring it along," Lily told her.

"Well, Bob certainly has good taste. No question about it. You're a handsome couple," Tammy complimented Lily and smiled to herself -- almost everyone is wearing old clothes tonight.

The Jamison's invitation was a brilliant idea.

Everyone enjoyed the hour to just relax with new friends. The conversations ranged from the lady's purchases to the men's day on the golf course. Michael was the perfect host, keeping glasses filled. Tammy enjoyed entertaining and had arranged for light hors d'oeuvres and a delicious cheese tray assortment delivered to their suite.

Tammy refreshed Joseph's glass and asked, "What exciting things did you two do today?"

"Actually, we stayed on board for the day and met a really nice couple at lunch. The buffet was worth the stay. The chef concentrated on specialties of the island. Florence was so happy to have a choice of seafood salads and I could have eaten the crab cakes all day. It was delicious. We ended up playing bridge with that couple for almost two hours." He put his arm around his wife. "Florence was the big winner."

Tammy's black-ribbed knit formal drew everyone s attention. There were only a few women that could get away with such a dress and she fit the bill. Kathleen's eyes were drawn to the red shell hanging from her hostess necklace.

"I'm glad we're all having a good time, but I have an announcement. I want you all to know that our bartender is sporting his one and only tux. I had to practically wrestle him to the floor to get him to put it on!"

Michael rolled his eyes and took another drink of his second glass of red wine.

"But, I still love him." Tammy laughed with everyone then put her arm around her husband and kissed him as she went on. "The mention of dress clothes reminds me of a story my dad told me. When he went on his first cruise he was young and knew nothing about the do's and don'ts of cruise clothing. Before leaving, he had shopped and was comfortable with what he had bought. One night he was invited to a captain's meet-the-passengers party. Dressed in his new chinos, a white shirt and sweater, Dad went off to the party. He was stunned, he told me, when he entered the captain's suite to see that he was the only one not in a tux."

"Oh, no," Lily said. "He must have felt awful."

"He did," Tammy admitted. "He was about to slip out just as the captain walked over to him, took his arm and, moving him around the room, and introduced him to the other passengers."

Joseph spoke up. "Now that's my kind of captain. A man who is a leader and doesn't forget who he is leading."

Tammy went on. "Dad was not prone to having an inferiority complex, but this time it was close, which only proves that clothes do not always make the man," Tammy concluded.

"That's what I keep telling her," Michael said. All of the men agreed, laughed, and raised their glasses.

Tammy looked at her watch. "Hey everyone, it's a quarter to eight. I think we had better get to the dining room. We don't want to miss anything."

They hurried down the hallway and all seven of them crowded into the elevator. Their waiter had told them the night before this was going to be a special night, honoring the 50th anniversary of Kingsley Cruise Line's first *Noble*. When they arrived at the dining room door, groups of people were mingling as they waited to enter. They heard unusual sounds from inside the dining room, but couldn't peek in. There was an uncharacteristic noise of tables and chairs being moved, an occasional sound of a loudspeaker system, and muted music from an indistinguishable era.

Lily spoke to the woman standing next to her. "Busy evening, isn't it. I wonder just what they have planned."

"I have no idea. I wonder, too. Must be special, though. I heard the Maitre d' asking people to wait before entering."

Within a few minutes the doors opened and the passengers began moving a few steps forward, just enough for Lily to see what the excitement was all about. When she realized what was going on, she was excited for Kathleen.

"Why don't you trade places with Kathleen?" she asked Bob. "It's her night." She reached for Kathleen's hand, anxious to move her closer. Kathleen could see a large monitor stretched across the end of the far wall of the dining room. Above the monitor was a large, colorful painting of the ship they were honoring – the first *Noble*. Below, a white banner with huge red letters announcing –

## 50TH ANNIVERSARY OF THE FIRST NOBLE -- 1964.

Kathleen starred at the wide screen of the monitor watching the videotape showing film clips and photos of the 1964 launching and sailing of *Noble* I.

"That's it! It's not 2014 style but, for me, nothing was better than that ship," she told Lily. "I'm *so glad* I'm here."

Lily watched her and saw the broad smile on her face and imagined what this moment must have been for Kathleen.

Tammy pushed her way through a group of white haired ladies waiting to be seated. "Whoops, sorry," she said as she bumped the cane of one of the passengers. "I have to get to my grandmother." Not a word of truth in what she said, but it did the trick.

Lily then grabbed Tammy's arm, moving her closer to Kathleen. "Look. It's the ship that Kathleen sailed on!"

"Oh, the love nest," Tammy joked, patting Kathleen on the shoulder.

"Enough jokes," Kathleen said, not looking away from the screen. "Watch. They are showing the interior of the ship." Kathleen was riveted to the screen, hoping for a miracle. Her mind was working overtime. *My God, am I going to see him? We spent so much time on that promenade deck.* She was twenty-five again. She searched each scene. *Just one more time. Please.*

Her memories were all over the place.

Michael gently guided Kathleen to the table in the center of the dining room. "Come on, Kathleen. Let's join the others at the table. You're the star of the hour. I think the captain is waiting for you."

Captain Freeland rose and shook her hand with both of his, so glad she had arrived at his table. "Welcome, Kathleen. I've been watching for you. Don't want you to miss a thing. Just sit back and enjoy yourself."

"It all just takes my breath away," Kathleen said as she joined the others and continued to stare at the screen.

Each table had been decorated with a small ship with "50" on the paper flag astern. Each place had a glossy commemorative copy of the 1964 season's brochure of *Noble* -- its launching, first itinerary, original menus, photos of a masquerade party, and a collage of special events on board.

"This is unbelievable. This is history revisited," Tammy said. "If only I had my camera crew here."

Kathleen was oblivious to anything but the monitor. *Oh, that video is moving so fast. Right past two photos. I hope they'll show it again. Could that possibly have been us?*

"Hmm," Tammy said. "See anyone you know?"

"I can't be sure. Maybe."

Tammy didn't bother her any further, realizing Kathleen was in a world of her own.

In time the screen went dark and the waiters served wine and took orders. Dinner conversation turned to questions about that first *Noble*. The men, more interested in the power and design of the ship, questioned the captain. Kathleen was filling the women in on details of the suites and the cruise clothes worn in the '60's.

"Look at those hairstyles," Tammy said, "and the length of the dresses!"

Familiar songs were piped-in throughout dinner -- everyone from Elvis, the Beatles, and Bob

Dylan to the Beach Boys, Ray Charles and Aretha Franklin. Singing in the dining room was unusual, but everyone did it tonight.

The captain asked Kathleen to tell people at his table something about what seemed familiar in the video.

"Everything," she exclaimed. "Fifty years have not wiped out any memory of that wonderful ship. *Noble* II is updated and beautiful, but the first *Noble* is etched in my mind in a very special way." She tapped her forehead, "It's here, forever, and I'm so glad you're all having a chance to enjoy the pictures."

Kathleen picked up the brochure at her place and turned the pages. Reminiscing. Stopping at each photo. Remembering places she and Kevin had been. *It was like a movie rerun. The deck chair where we first met. Oh, my God.* Then she stopped turning the pages and focused on one photo. *That's where he sat in the dining room. Wish he'd been there when they took that picture. The Twist? He danced better than me. He said that wasn't true, but it was. There's our little table in the bar! Everything started there!*

On the very last page there was a photo of a group of passengers standing at the early morning outdoor breakfast table. Her mouth went dry. *That's him.* She had found him. *I know it's him. That's how he stood. Those are his white deck shoes. I'm sure!* She just couldn't believe it.

Tammy noticed tears on Kathleen's cheeks. "Are you alright," she asked from across the table.

Kathleen closed the brochure. "I'm fine. Really."

"Are you sure?"

"Yes, I guess. It's all the excitement. This party. The film. Going back all those years. Memories get to me sometimes." Kathleen put the brochure down, noticing everyone's concern, "I'm fine."

In reality, for that moment, she wasn't fine. Her heart was beating faster than usual. *I better sit still for a minute,* she thought. *Have to get rid of this dizziness. Why's my mouth so dry?* She picked up her glass of water, sipped, and just for a moment she closed her eyes.

Dessert was served. Everyone continued talking about the *Noble* pictures and the music of the sixties. There were so many questions about that decade. They were curious about what Kathleen had experienced on that first *Noble* cruise. Though feeling better now, their questions, her answers, and the side conversations were a blur. Her focus was Kevin.

Tammy, looking at everyone, said, "I was so impressed with that presentation. Boy, you were lucky to be part of that cruise. You can tell that there must have been lots and lots of hours of research involved in producing it. Wish it was me!"

"That video makes your cruise look so exciting. Did you ever get a chance to rest?" Lily asked.

"Not much."

Lily noticed that Kathleen was brief.

Tammy saved the moment. "It was special, but where do we go from here? I'm too pumped up to turn in yet. Suggestions?"

"Before you leave the dining room," the captain proposed, "you should stop by the table to the right of the entrance. You're in for a surprise."

Curiosity got the best of everyone. Dinner over, they moved on to see what he had referred to. And they were surprised. Spread out on a table was the memorabilia that Kathleen had brought on the cruise and earlier left at the purser's office as a donation to Kinsley Cruise Line. Unknown to Kathleen, the public relations office had set up a special display to commemorate *Noble*. In the center of the large, round table was a printed card –

## MEMORIES DO NOT DIE
## YOU HOLD ON TO THEM FOREVER

And below it –

### Donated by
### KATHLEEN O'CONNELL
### INAUGURAL *NOBLE* CRUISE -- 1964

Diners were crowded around the table enjoying her tribute to the past. There was just one thing that she had found in the attic that she didn't share – "the note."

Tammy couldn't believe the fact that Kathleen had told no one about this presentation. "Where in the world did you find all this stuff?" she asked.

"Stuck away in my attic."

Lily had tears in her eyes when she saw what her friend had held on to. She knew it had to have been important to her.

The moment had affected them all. Kathleen's memories of the first cruise of *Noble* respectfully arranged on a *Noble II* table. She was happy that she had brought them, but needed to move on.

## CHAPTER 10

Kathleen surprised everyone. "Before we turn in, let's all go to the casino at the end of this deck and try our luck." *Memories are out for a while. I've got to get over this mood. Everyone has made this night so special for me.*

"I knew you were my girl," Lily said, putting her arm around Kathleen and giving her a hug. "Let's live it up."

Bob looked at Lily and winked. "What do you say we try the tables? I feel lucky tonight."

"No way!" Lily shook her head. "You men can get involved in that if you want. The slots are my cup of tea. How about you, girls?"

They all agreed, and walked down the deck toward the casino. Soon they heard the sound of slot machines paying off and voices of excited winners. The room was in full swing. The women moved quickly to find an empty machine, while the men eased their way between roulette players and got their chips placed.

Kathleen sat down at a slot machine ironically called "Fantasy Cruise." Within a few minutes of making one-dollar bets, three cruise ships appeared on her screen. "Free Spin" flashed before her on the slot machine screen and a loud ship's bell continued to ring from the machine. She had won ten free spins and her total winnings kept increasing.

"Oh my gosh, I won eighty-five dollars!" Kathleen fed the machine continuously for the next hour, never betting more than a dollar. Additional winnings came and went, but she was having a good time.

"Hey, look at this," Lily called excitedly to Tammy. Her machine, "Flaming Ice," came up showing five icebergs with bright flames atop each, melting the ice. Winning numbers rose as the icebergs melted. More bells rang and "BIG WINNER" spread across the screen. When the game finished, Lily had won five hundred dollars.

She walked over to Bob to tell him of her new found wealth. "How are you guys doing?"

"Well, I keep coming in second with each spin." Bob laughed and pointed to Michael's chip stack. "Now he's got a good pile of chips. But I'm having a good time, even though I'm not winning."

Lily smiled. "You're a good sport, honey."

Michael slapped Bob on the back. "At least the bar is still open."

Joseph and Florence watched the excitement but didn't play, and after about a half-hour they called it a night.

"Oh my gosh, look!" Lily shouted, pounding on Tammy's arm. The cheering crowd around Lily was so large and so loud that it drew even more people.

"How much? How much?" Tammy yelled over the excitement in the small casino room.

"I don't know yet," Lily screamed back. "It just keeps paying, but it's got to be huge." It was another minute before the loud bells and bright flashing lights stopped. Lily excitedly pointed at the screen. "Look. $200."

Tammy leaned over and took a closer look. "No. Look. There's another zero. That's $2,000. And you, my dear, are a winner again!"

Kathleen cashed out and walked over to where everyone was cheering, but Lily had a strange look on her face. "What happened, Lily?" Kathleen asked, concerned there might be a problem.

Tammy jumped in. "She just won $2,000 and she was only playing a dollar at a time! First the Mega Million lottery and now another $2,000 dollars." Tammy hugged Lily. "Alright, tell us how you do it. I haven't had any luck. Zero."

Back at the tables Bob, who had definitely not been winning, said to Michael, "Let's go see which of the girls hit the jackpot." He looked over and saw his wife was getting all of the attention. He elbowed Michael. "Hey. It's Lily."

Bob pushed his way through the lingering group of people, finally reaching Lily. "What's happening, honey?"

Lily grabbed his hand. "You won't believe it. I did it again. I just won $2,000 dollars."

"Well, moneybags, for some reason dollars seem to love you," Bob joked, hugging his wife. "Try it again and let's share!"

Everyone around them laughed. Lily cautiously played five more dollars. "No luck. That's it. I'm done," she announced as she cashed out. "Expecting more would be tempting fate."

"This has really been a great day," Bob said, reaching for Lily's hand as they started walking toward the elevator along with Kathleen.

"Except for my bogey on the fifth green," Michael kidded as he and Tammy joined the others.

"And my feeding a month s grocery money into a 'Felix Flops' machine," Tammy said. "Can you imagine that name for a slot machine? Should have been 'Tammy Trips'. I got skunked."

Kathleen laughed. "A lovely cocktail party. A delicious dinner. A great celebration. And even winning at the casino." She turned to Tammy. "What more could you ask for. A memorable evening for us all."

"Now we need a good night's sleep," Tammy told them. "Tomorrow is our last day in St. Thomas. I'm going to turn in and get my beauty sleep."

The group followed Tammy's lead. As they walked to the elevators, Kathleen kept fiddling with her bracelets. She thought about the evening. What was it that Tammy had said about keep looking around the corner?

# CHAPTER 11

$\mathcal{B}$y 8:00 am Kathleen had settled out on Promenade Deck. The sun was not quite up yet and a chilly sea breeze blew in. A deck waiter brought her a steamy cup of coffee from the early morning snack bar that was set up for the walkers and joggers. With a deck blanket wrapped around her, Kathleen lay back with the coffee cup warming her hands and enjoyed the moment. She was surprised to see Lily and Bob approaching her.

"Hi. You're up nice and early. It's kind of chilly out here, isn't it?" Lily said.

"Yes, I'm just going to finish my coffee and then get an early start." Kathleen pulled her blanket closer. "It should warm up pretty quick. The TV said it is to be a beautiful day."

"Good. Where are you going?" Bob asked.

"I'm going out to the beach. Every time I get down here, I go back to search for unusual shells. I have quite a collection. What are you folks up to?"

"We're going duty free shopping! Bob needs a new camera. Hope we can find one he likes. Now that we have the casino winnings, we can live dangerously."

Bob spoke up quickly. "Remember her words, Kathleen."

Kathleen laughed. "Well, have fun and good luck." Another half hour passed before she was in line to disembark.

She noticed Tammy and Michael were already down on the dock. They waved up to her and she went down the ramp to meet them. Tammy was dressed in a short-sleeved light blue linen blouse and navy Bermudas.

"Hey, how about joining us?" Tammy asked. "We're off to the University of the Virgin Islands at the other end of the island. Michael wants to talk to the head of the environmental science department about his theory and his proposed book."

"That would be fun, but I'm headed for the beach," Kathleen told them.

"That sounds good too, and you sure have perfect weather. Incidentally, I love your beach bag," Tammy observed.

"I got it at Bloomingdales. It comes in all colors. You might want to check them out when you get back to the city."

Tammy nodded. "It looks like Florence and Joseph are staying on board. Joseph said that the ship's library has a fairly large book collection and that the chairs were very comfortable."

"Well, good. I saw them just before I left the ship and they were heading in that direction," Kathleen said.

Michael looked at his watch. "If we're going to be back before four, we had better get started. I'd like to be on board when the ship sails."

"You don't think it would be fun to swim out to it?" Tammy laughed and turned to Kathleen. "I just couldn't help it."

They agreed to meet back on the ship in the Shell Lounge for a drink before dinner. Tammy and Michael walked to the cabstand a block away and were off to the university.

Kathleen wanted to get to the beach before high tide. She hailed a taxi. It was hot and stuffy, so she quickly put the windows down to enjoy the cooling breeze. As they drove along, children smiled and waved to her as they walked along the side of the road on their way to school. Kathleen waved back.

She knew the areas well. St Thomas had been a favorite destination for clients. Returning to the area today was not about clients. It was about Kevin.

She was enjoying the quiet ride when suddenly she noticed a tall, thin man in a plaid shirt and jeans walking slowly on the other side of the road. His hair was gray and patches of red were visible even from the cab. *Oh God.* She caught her breath. *Maybe. Would Kevin's hair be grey now? This is crazy, but I've got to know.*

"Stop here, please, just for a minute," she told the driver. He immediately pulled over and Kathleen got out. Slowly, she crossed the street and moved toward the man.

"Kevin?" she called. She held her breath until he turned around. Almost immediately she knew it was not Kevin. He could not possibly have changed that much. She made her apologies, saying she had mistaken him for an old friend. He nodded and continued on.

*I should have known better*, she thought, and returned to the taxi. Kathleen asked the driver to drive slowly along the beach. She was searching. She had noticed a small hotel in the distance. "Stop," she cried out. "Here it is." The driver skidded over the blown sand on the road as he quickly pulled to the curb.

*I was right. This is our beach. And I can't believe the hotel is still here fifty years later!* She paid the driver, took off her light sandals, and kicked the soft sand as she walked along the top of the grass-covered dunes. She stopped and looked down at the broad white beach, remembering.

A light breeze gently blew her hair, reminding her of another windy day. Kevin had laughed as she fought to keep her hair out of her eyes and told her she looked beautiful.

Kathleen moved over to a small cove, dropped her bag, and immediately walked down to the water. She was so happy to see that it was low tide. Several seagulls sailed above, while others pecked at the sand at the water line, searching for their morning treat before the tide came in.

Kathleen splashed the water as it slowly worked its way up the shore. So happy that she was here, she spread her arms out, laughed, and rushed along the damp shoreline, thinking how good it was to be here again. It made her feel younger and more alive, but lonesome, too. As she walked through the foamy water, she found a few unusual shells and a couple of red pieces of sea glass. *These are really unusual,* she thought. *Usually brown or transparent or green -- not red. This is the most wonderful place in the world.* She clutched the sea glass to her chest and looked down the beach. *Our beach. Unspoiled. Full of memories and questions. Since that old hotel survived, maybe it's not to late for us. Funny, those fifty years are just blown away when I am here.*

Returning to the cove, Kathleen picked up her beach bag, pulled out a small blanket, and laid it out. She sat down, looking over her shells and sea glass before putting them in her bag then laid back. In no time she was asleep, but not for long. An insistent fly decided to buzz her nose. She sat up and tried batting it away, but the fly was insistent and they continued their duel.

The sun had grown hot. When she was sixteen, she found the hot sun was the means to a wonderful tan. A little burn first and then the tan. Now, she wasn't after a burn or a tan, just time to remember their beach. Kathleen had grown thirsty from her walk in the strong sun and looked in her bag for a bottle of water. *Oh, no. I left it on the deck.* Remembering the small hotel, she stuffed her sandals and towels away and headed up the beach.

Fifty years ago the hotel had been the only spot available for food and drinks in the area. As she approached the entrance, Kathleen thought, *this has surely changed. A new paint job would help. It's lost its charm; it's just run-down now.* She shook her head. *Years can do that to us all.*

She slipped into her sandals and stepped inside the door. No sooner had she entered than someone called her name.

She froze for a moment, hearing a man's voice. A millisecond. August 10, 1964, flashed through her head. *Our beach. Our sand. Our love.* She whipped around, hoping.

"Hey, Kathleen, never expected to see you out here in God's country." It was Jim, the captain's son.

Instantly, her hope it might be Kevin evaporated.

Jim was holding hands with a very pretty blond girl outside the coffee shop in the lobby of the hotel. Kathleen recognized her as his girlfriend, Abby, whom she had meet on board. They were both wearing white tennis shorts and polo shirts.

"We've been playing a couple of sets of tennis nearby. You'll have to forgive the way we look."

Once more Kathleen thought how really pretty Jim's girlfriend was. "You two looked great."

"Are you here for lunch?" Jim asked.

"I'm just here for a bottle of water. Every time I come to St. Thomas, I head for this beach. I collect shells and sea glass. It's a great place to find unusual examples. But I forgot how hot it can be out there."

"Well, come on and join us. We're going to the coffee shop for lunch. The last time I was here I had the most incredible cheeseburger. I want Abby to try one. They added some special sauce."

"Sounds tempting but you two go ahead. Thanks for asking me though."

"No, you don't." Jim took Kathleen's arm. "You're coming with us. The beach will still be there in an hour."

Kathleen didn't resist.

The coffee shop was definitely a step up from the outside of the building. Bright Caribbean colors were everywhere and each table had fresh tropical flowers. At the windows were cafe curtains in a bold red and yellow pattern. They found a circular booth tucked away at the end of the room.

After Jim's cheeseburger rave, they all decided to try one. When they were settled and the order had been taken, Abby turned to Kathleen. "I'm so glad to be able to talk with you. Jim told me about the dragnet it took to find you."

"I don't know about a dragnet, but I surely am glad that they found me. This cruise has been so great."

Knowing that Kathleen had been in the travel business, they asked lots of questions about places that they had never visited. Kathleen thought there might be a honeymoon in their future. It was fun to see their interest in learning about uncommon destinations. Places that the masses had missed.

Not wanting to be the focus of the conversation, she asked Jim to tell her something of himself. *Hmm*, she wondered, *am I beginning to sound like Tammy?*

"Well, let's see if I can fill you in a little on my wild and crazy existence. For the last fifteen years, the Navy has been my life."

Abby nudged him. "And what about me?"

"Oh, that too, right." He laughed and returned the nudge. "Most of the time I have drawn good duty. No complaints." He turned to Abby. "Your turn now."

"My turn, well, okay. I'd love to tell you about my fantastic job, but I don't have one right now," Abby said. "Jim's the exciting part of my life. The navy claims him more than I like but that's his career. Getting together doesn't happen often enough so when his leave came up, we jumped at the chance to be together on *Noble* two," Abby smiled. In a stage whisper to Kathleen, she added, "He is at the table with his dad for meals, but I have claimed his free time. Think you can guess I'll take seeing him however and whenever I can."

"Yes. It's hard when you're apart but that makes your together time more special," Kathleen remembered.

"It does, Mrs. O'Connell. You sound as though you've been there. Are you a navy wife?"

"I was married once long ago. In fact, yes, my husband was in the navy, but that was back in the '60's. I remember a couple of long tours that he had in the Mediterranean. It seemed as though he was gone forever. Ironically, he died while he was on land. So, I know what you're feeling," Kathleen agreed.

"Not fair," Abby said as she reached for Kathleen's hand. Did you re-marry?"

"No, I didn't."

"Come close?"

"Sort of. As a matter of fact on my first cruise on the first *Noble*, I met a handsome man. We had a wonderful time together. Watch out, Abby, or you'll be stuck sitting here and hearing the story of my life."

"Come on, Kathleen, don't stop now," Abby encouraged.

Kathleen turned to Jim. "I'm not going to get carried away but, as a matter of fact, he was about to become navy, too."

Abby perked up. "We're you engaged?"

"Actually, we might have been. That possibility ended at the dock in New York. He had to rush off to his daughter who had been hit by a car."

Abby leaned forward. "Oh, I'm sorry. So how did you two get back together?"

"We didn't."

"What?" Jim asked.

"Well, it never dawned on us that we would be separated. No addresses or phone numbers came up. That would have probably happened before we left the ship, but by morning he was gone. Back to his daughter."

"That's terrible," Abby said.

"I tried to find him and I'm sure he tried to find me. I couldn't get information from the Kingsley Cruise Line regarding any personal information. I even called navy personnel. They wouldn't give me any help and…"

Jim interrupted. "No surprise there."

Kathleen nodded and continued. "I suppose. I did all I could but there were nothing but dead ends. But, that was 50 years ago."

"Life isn't always fair," Abby said and gave Kathleen a hug.

*What nice kids,* Kathleen thought. *St. Thomas creates special moments even now. I got carried away and I've taken too much of their time.*

"Thank you so much for letting me join you. I want to get back in the sun for a little while. You two kids have been so much fun for me to be with. Now enjoy the rest of the day." Kathleen grabbed the check,

IF…

paid at the counter, and waved to Jim and Abby who were smiling and waving to her as she left.

Returning to the empty beach, she noticed high tide was creeping in. Dropping her bag near the dunes, she hurried down the smooth white sand. *This is probably the last time I'll share this beach with you, Kevin. I didn't know how important our time here was.* While the next wave crept up, covering her feet, she said quietly, "I really did love you."

A few minutes later she turned, reluctantly, and began walking back up the beach, re-tracing her footsteps. A family of sand crabs crossing in front of her distracted her thoughts. As she watched them go down the beach, she noticed another set of footprints leading to the sand dunes.

*I don't get it. I know there weren't footprints here a few minutes ago.* Kathleen looked up and down the beach. No one. *That couldn't be -- no.* She looked around again. *This is way too mysterious.*

She continued on to her bag and as she leaned over to pick it up saw something red sticking out of the sand. Kathleen picked it up. *A red shell. My God. This is weird.* Now nervous, she thought, *I need to leave here and get back to the ship.* Kathleen placed the shell in the side pocket of her bag. "I don't know what's going on, but I'll save it for you, Kevin," she whispered.

There had been a few taxis in the driveway when she had left the hotel earlier. Kathleen hoped

113

they were still there. Quickly she walked through the sand to the service entrance of the hotel. *Thank goodness, there's still one here.* The heavy-set taxi driver, his shirt unbuttoned and leaning against his vehicle, smoking, was smiling.

Kathleen approached him. "I'd like a ride back to the to my ship in Charlotte Amalie."

"I've been hoping for a rider, ma'am, I'll get you there." The taxi driver casually flicked his cigarette away and nonchalantly opened the door for her. As they drove away, she looked back at the beach. *Good-bye.* She wondered if she would be back again. She didn't know.

## CHAPTER 12

The new friends had returned to the ship early. As arranged earlier, they met in the Shell Lounge on Starlight Deck for a drink at the end of the afternoon. They were all anxious to talk about how the last day in St. Thomas had gone. They ordered drinks and sat back, and the chatter began.

"Kathleen how did your day at the beach go?" Tammy asked.

"I had a great time. While I was there, I stopped at a hotel I had visited 50 years ago. First, I was surprised it was still standing. And then as I walked in to the lobby, our tablemate, Jim, and his girl, Abby, were there. We had a wonderful lunch together and most of our time we discussed life in the navy."

Kathleen felt better about not sharing her beach visit or finding a red shell. There were certain things in life that are too intimate to share with others.

"He seems like such a nice boy," Lily said.

Tammy raised her vodka tonic and said, "It's a shame he's so young!"

Michael looked at his wife, not smiling. "Hmm?"

"Oh, 'hmm' yourself. You know you're safe. Who else would I ever want to be with except someone who is an authority on cow manure and my electric bill?"

115

Hilarity echoed throughout the bar.

Michael followed up. "My wife's fantasies aside, we had a good time at the university. I had an important discussion with the chair of the environmental science department." He shifted in his chair. "Initially, he was concerned about a couple of issue, but I feel that was all straightened out."

"Yes, dear. I had the best part of the afternoon. You were sweating away discussing cow manure while I was walking around campus, which has a magnificent view of the Caribbean. What a beautiful place," Tammy said.

They all exchanged their experiences for the next two hours at dinner. Jokes flew. Stories unfolded. By the time dinner was over, everyone was exhausted from the full day and returned to their suites.

That night, the ship departed from St. Thomas, sailing on to its next port, St. Martin. At breakfast the captain suggested everyone might enjoy a briefing of the next island they were to visit. "It is customary for us to have someone come aboard on arrival at St. Martin to tell you of their own particular island and what it offers the cruise visitor. It's interesting and saves you from wandering around, uncertain of where to go."

Most of Kathleen's group of friends thought it was a great idea.

"I think Florence and I will not join you," Joseph told them. "We have visited the island several times and so I think we will stay aboard. Don't you miss it, though. It's a real treat."

"And I think I won't attend the briefing either, Dad," Jim told his father. "Abby had visited St. Martin with her brother, her mother, and dad last year. She wants me to see the area she and her brother found. We are going to rent horses and ride the mountain trails out to where she said was one of the most beautiful deserted beaches she had ever seen. She convinced me I'd love it. We're going."

"She's right," Kathleen remembered. "I recall that in some brochure I read. There is a romantic and hidden area."

"Well, I've never visited the island and I think the briefing would be good for me," Tammy was up and ready to go. "Anyone else coming?"

"We are." Lily and Bob joined her, as did Kathleen.

A group had gathered in one of the larger lounges and a guide from a local tourist agency was there arranging brochures of St. Martin.

"Good morning," the young woman said. "I'm so glad so many of you could join me. I know you are anxious to go ashore so I'll make this brief. I like to tell visitors something of my St. Martin and what it has to offer them. And please feel free to speak up if you have any questions."

"St. Martin was both French and Dutch. Sort of a split personality. We're known as the gourmet capital of the Caribbean. You're in for a big surprise. My favorite is Coconut Shrimp. And I'll bet some of you will be glad to hear you can also have hamburger and enormous grilled fish sandwiches."

Lily beamed when the speaker went on to mention that the island was duty free. She spoke up. "Is there anything special to shop for?"

"A very good question. You don't want to miss the jewelry shops. And if you love fine linens - bedding, hand cut tablecloths, and French perfumes make your way over to the French section of the island. Their shops are what you might call fashionable. Be sure to go to the town of Margot, the French capital. It has an aura -- European ambience some say."

Tammy blurted out, "*Tres bien.*"

"*Vous avez raison, madam,*" the guide responded smiling. "And the Dutch side will offer you turquoise waters, sparkling beaches, and of course, sailing, jet skiing, and night life. Sadly, I think you will be departing before you can take advantage in the evening of the casinos and a special taste of their nightlife. Yes, and you'll find special foods and shopping everywhere."

The guide continued, "I see that there are several men here this morning. I am sure that you will

118

be glad to know that you can purchase Cuban cigars on the island."

Bob leaned over to Michael, "Hmm, guy gifts!"

"Moving on from shopping, our beaches are beautiful -- pure white sand. If you like snorkeling or scuba diving, don't leave without an hour or two beneath our clear blue waters. And there are boat rentals. They're out there waiting for you on the waterfront. Whatever you do, you're in for a treat," she said. The guide completed her briefing and thanked them for coming.

Everyone had a full day on the island and they made the most of it before they had to sail on.

As the cruise continued to Barbados and Antiqua, it was a perfect sailing with wonderful visits. The itinerary on this new ship was well chosen - each island a little different, yet rewarding in its own way.

Late in the afternoon after their day visiting Barbados, Kathleen and Tammy returned to the ship and went into the art gallery where they were served tea. Over the past five days, they had become quite close. Their conversations progressed from simple social greetings the first day to better understanding each other.

"This is really some cruise, isn't it?" Tammy asked Kathleen as they sat down at a table next to a wide window. The afternoon sun cast a large silhouette of the ship on the flat sea.

Kathleen leaned back and in a calm voice said, "It has been wonderful. I'm so thankful for this second opportunity. You know, I'm dwelling on the past more than I should, but each island has its own story for me. It's hard to keep it all inside sometimes."

Tammy said softly, "Well, the best way to take care of that is to tell a friend – here I am."

Kathleen thought for a moment as she slowly had a sip of her tea. "Okay. I trust you, but this is strictly between you and me. As you thought before, I met a man on the original *Noble*."

"There was something about what you said while we were having drinks at the 1812 Hotel. It sounded as though you showed more than clients around St. Thomas. Almost as though you were romantically reminiscing."

Kathleen laughed. "You got me. I was."

"So share a little."

"Well, he was so very nice. I liked him right away. We met on deck. We talked then we talked some more. This could make for a successful film for you some day."

"Let me get my pad of paper out. Where's a camera when you need one?" Tammy kidded.

"I need to get my makeup on first," Kathleen said, going along with Tammy's quip. "We were not assigned to the same table at meals, but the rest of our days we were inseparable. We were always the first off the ship and the last back on in most occasions. We wanted a little distance from others and always tried to find some quiet time together."

"You were such a lucky lady."

"I remember one port in particular. It was the private island owned by the Kingsley line. We were there only for one day, but one I'll never forget. For some reason I do recall not everyone on board wanted to go ashore. Maybe I only had eyes for him and couldn't see the others."

Tammy couldn't resist. "That's corny, but cute, Kathleen."

"The cruise line hosted a beach party and the island was prepared for the visitors. Beach chairs, umbrellas, and floating mats were waiting for us. And…what did we eat?" Kathleen hesitated, knitting her brows as she tried to recall. "Oh, I know. Some unique island style barbecue, an all-you-can-eat buffet. I think we had to pay for drinks, but that was all. I'm not sure what we did besides eat and drink." Her eyes opened wide. "Oh. A conga line. I hadn't remembered that for 50 years!"

Tammy picked up her cup. "Oh, you kid. You should lead a line on the boat. I'll talk to the cruise director about that."

"I could then, not now. Don't you dare say anything." Kathleen thought more about that day. "I know we did something else. We were there all afternoon. Maybe snorkeling. Uh, Frisbee? Certainly swimming. I think we went back to the ship right after

121

swimming. He said something like…" Kathleen wrinkled her nose. "…It will be like our own private yacht with so many people on shore. And he was right."

"What a great story. You had yourself quite a time. This must really be a wonderful walk down memory lane for you."

"It was, but it's not the same, Tammy."

They heard laughter outside the gallery as Lily, Bob, and Michael walked in. "So, this is where you girls have been hiding. We've been looking all over for you. Thought you went skeet shooting or something," Michael said.

"No dear. No guns. Way too noisy for my tender ears and I might spill my drink," Tammy admitted. "Besides there are other things to do here."

"I know that's true." He turned to the others. "She's up early, probably before the captain, and off to the fitness center."

"Hey. I' m always up early. I go to the gym, which is pretty challenging. Then off to the spa. A girl's got to pamper herself once in a while, you know."

Michael frowned. "I do know. I have to get up with you to turn off your alarm clock."

Everyone laughed.

"Lily, why don't you join me some morning?" Tammy asked.

"My idea of exercise is a nice swim and then an equally nice long, cool drink while I lay in the sun. Now that's a vacation," Lily smiled.

Kathleen agreed. "There are some days when a vodka tonic and sunlight make a great mix. How about you men?"

Bob jumped in. "Oh, I love a good pedicure, but I have trouble deciding what color I want my toes painted."

"Okay, Bob," Lily said as she touched his arm. "I need to get ready for dinner. We only have two more evenings before we go back to the real world. Will you all excuse us?"

After another five-star dinner at the captain's table, everyone left for the main lounge for the evening's entertainment. There was to be a special musical presentation and there wasn't an empty seat in the house.

The cruise director came out on stage. "Tonight in keeping with this commemorative cruise, the Kingsley Cruise Line has a special program for you. Music from Broadway shows of 1964 -- Hello Dolly, High Spirits, Fade Out, Fade In, Fiddler on the Roof, and Funny Girl."

Enthusiastic applause followed.

"That's not all," he continued, "some of our crew members, stewards, cooks, waiters, and others will entertain you with their great voices. We know they sing well because each has been heard in our passageways, our kitchens, and in our showers. We hope you enjoy the evening."

The music started up and began with the maître d' walking out, singing, "If I Were a Rich Man." Everyone laughed and no one missed the innuendo from the man who had been tipped by all the passengers at one time or another in the dining room.

During the evening, most of the audience sang along. Kathleen, Tammy, Michael, Lily, Bob, even Florence and Joseph joined right in. Halfway through the program, Kathleen's stewardess, Caitlyn, came out on stage.

Kathleen leaned over to Lily. "She's my stewardess. Isn't she cute?"

The cruise director introduced Caitlyn's song from Funny Girl and the lights dimmed as she began

All had been going well for Kathleen. She knew almost all of the songs and was having a wonderful time -- until Caitlyn's words struck home –

> *Oh, my man, I love him so*
> *He'll never know*
> *All my life is just despair*
> *But I don't care…*

Kathleen sat frozen. *Our song. Kevin said this could be our song.* She squeezed her hands tightly.

*…When he takes me in his arms.*
*The world is bright, alright…*

By the time the lyrics reached

*For whatever my man is*
*I am his forever more…*

"I think this is even better than Broadway," Lily whispered.

Kathleen never heard Lily. She was out of her chair and on her way back to her suite, tears streaming down her cheeks. A sleepless night of memories returned.

# CHAPTER 13

There was just one stop left on the itinerary – San Juan. It was a short one, but an important one for Kathleen. After breakfast the ship's passengers were given an informative briefing by one of the ship's Staff.

Still sitting at their table, Tammy asked Kathleen if she would join them when they reached port. She and Michael were taking a taxi into the city. "I'm sure you have been there many times, Kathleen, but come on along anyway. Michael has to pick up some information for his book. While he's doing that we can find a really good restaurant. Native Puerto Rican food is wonderful. I've flown down here several times and know a couple of special little places away from tourists. How about it?"

"You tempt me Tammy, but I have some things I have to do here in Old San Juan and our stop is short. Why don't you ask Lily and Bob? Bet they would enjoy going with you."

Tammy looked disappointed Kathleen couldn't join them, but she understood and told her to make the most of the time she had.

When the ship docked in Old San Juan, Kathleen was anxious to leave as soon as possible. A half hour later she walked into El Convento Hotel and sat in the lovely courtyard, ordering a glass of

Chardonnay. *Alright*, she thought, *this is my time. I can wallow in remembering without boring anyone. She lifted her glass and toasted the moment. To you, Kevin. I loved you. This cruise brings back all of our great times. What could have happened? I had forgotten so much, but not our times here.* She looked around. *To me it's as beautiful now as it was then. Just one more thing I need to do for us.*

Kathleen finished her drink and retraced their steps, walking to the San Juan Batista Cathedral. She knelt and said a prayer, then left the cathedral, still with a heavy heart, and walked along the narrow cobble-stoned streets to the El Morro Fortress. She kept processing their days together. *It would mean so much. I hope our memory is still there.* She hurried her steps and prepared herself for disappointment. *So many years have passed.*

As she arrived at the Fortress, she crossed her fingers. *I hope it's still here.* She wandered along the walkways, searching. Just about ready to give up, she found it. She kneeled down and rubbed her hand over the letters. *KO - KJ.* "It's still here, Kevin," she whispered. *Remember? Concrete was wet. You sneaked under the rope with my nail file. I wish our love had lasted as long as our initials.*

An elderly guard stopped and cleared his throat.

Kathleen started to get up, the man reaching out to help her. "Oh, I'm sorry. Just an old memory."

He smiled. "Old memories are important." He tipped his hat and shuffled on.

The last full day aboard ship was always busy. Everyone trying to make up for lost time. Kathleen returned to the ship, joining those in the crowded gift shop. Lists were out and passengers checking off names as they shopped for friends and relatives, some for their bosses. There was a tennis bracelet that had caught Kathleen's eye several days earlier. She thought Lexi would like it and she bought it.

Only guests who had made appointments at the spa in advance got in. The beauty salon chairs filled with those wanting to look their best. Tomorrow morning they would arrive back in New York City and return to the real world.

Before getting ready for dinner, Kathleen walked out to the veranda, watching the sky change color as the sun began to dip into the horizon. She could almost feel Kevin putting his arm around her that last night -- fifty years ago. *If we'd only been together when he got word of his daughter's car accident and had not already gone to our staterooms after dinner.* Tears welled up. *This is a different ship and a different time, but the same memory.* Kathleen took a deep breath. *I need to pull myself together and get ready for dinner.*

Kathleen had prepared for this. Among the clothes that she had packed was a long chiffon dress --

pale blue. It was the dress she had put away after the first *Noble* cruise, for later. Going through the attic for a second time, she had found it and was amazed that the dress had withstood the years of waiting. *What a sentimental fool I am. It doesn't matter. I'm going to wear it anyway. I have a feeling some would question my sanity for holding on to the dress. Who cares -- not many of us get a second chance like this.* She was determined she was not going to let convention get in her way. *I'm alive and I'm reliving a dream. Not just as I thought it would play out -- but who knows?*

Kathleen finished dressing. She always had mixed feelings at this point on the cruise -- excited by what she remembered was the pinnacle of the chef's work and disappointed the cruise would soon be over. The last dinner was always one that passengers remembered. A tradition in cruising.

The Captain's Group, as they became known to each other, met in the bar on their deck for the last time. It was a subdued crowd. Time was running out. They would miss the friendships they had made and wanted just one more time to share before the ship docked in the morning.

"Hey, everybody, why so quiet?" Tammy had just joined the group and felt the same way the rest of them did, but was determined not to let the evening fall flat. "Is this the way you all acted on that last night

129

fifty years ago, Kathleen?" She turned to her friend for help in keeping the conversation going.

Kathleen looked down at her evening bag, taking a moment to answer. "No, we were busy and excited." They could see that Kathleen was thinking about that last trip.

"Here, here," Michael said, trying to cheer the group up. "Let's drink to that and toast to Kathleen's happy memories."

Kathleen thought, *I know that they would have liked Kevin and he would have like them.*

"You're right, Michael," Bob said. "Maybe we could sing some Broadway musical numbers."

"Oh, no. Don't you dare. It's enough hearing you at home. Please don't make our friends suffer," Lily laughed.

Florence pointed to her husband. "Ditto for you, Joseph."

Joseph agreed. "You're right dear. Let's go to dinner."


Everyone wanted to look their best tonight, their last night. Ladies sparkled in their jewelry. Men looked handsome in their tux. It was like a Hollywood movie. The reality of tomorrow was tucked away and tonight the clock stood still.

The dining room was a little quieter than usual throughout the dinner hour. At the end of the sumptuous meal the lights dimmed. Everyone looked toward the floor-to-ceiling glass doors as they slowly folded back. From behind them on the dimmed staircases came the waiters, on either side of a dramatic waterfall, carrying the traditional flaming Baked Alaska glowing upon their trays. It was such a beautiful glittering sight, such a special moment. Cheers spontaneously erupted.

The music of Auld Lang Syne filled the air. Everyone stood and joined in singing. Many clasped the hand of the person next to them. Husbands put their arm around their wives. Slowly the waiters moved across the room, placing their tray in the center of each table. The dining room lights dimmed further, leaving only a candlelit moment. Silence again 'til the room once more brightened and the Baked Alaska was served.

This was the high point of the cruise. It ended the dinner hour in a stately manner. In a matter of hours, the ship would dock at New York's Pier Nine. Although the passengers were going home, they would always carry the memory of this night with them.

"Well, Captain Freeman, you certainly know how to give a party!" Tammy said, patting him on his sleeve. Everyone agreed with Tammy's unusual thanks.

"My greatest wish is that you remember the ship -- and me. When I am the host, I indeed enjoy my guests. This was special, though. I felt that I was entertaining my friends."

131

Murmurs of understanding rippled around the table.

Making the best of their last evening, passengers went to a bar or back to the casino. The younger passengers stayed up into the early hours, again dancing to live music or singing at the karaoke bar.

Breakfast the next morning hummed. Telephone numbers and email addresses circulated around the table. Everyone promised they would be in touch and talked of a reunion once a year.

Passengers disembarked mid-morning and made their way through customs. Henry was waiting for Kathleen at the curb and greeted her with a big smile. The ride to Connecticut was conversational.

"Mrs. O'Connell, I must tell you that Samantha Ann had a wonderful birthday and your present contributed to her computer tablet filled with games she could play. That was very special to her."

"That's great, Henry. I hope she'll enjoy it. Children need to enjoy their youth."

Kathleen told him about her cruise all the way to her front door.

## CHAPTER 14

As soon as Kathleen walked in, she called her sister. "Hi, Lex. I'm home."

"Welcome home. How are you?"

"Excited and happy. We've got to get together. I have so much to tell you."

"And I want to hear it all. I know you've got a lot to do, but how about breakfast tomorrow morning?"

"Great. I can do whatever, whenever. How about late morning? Eleven work?"

"Eleven is good -- at the usual place. See you then."

Kathleen occupied the rest of her day unpacking, setting aside clothes for the cleaners, doing a little housework, grocery shopping, and then went next door to pick up Mabel. Then, so anxious to see Lexi, she arrived at the restaurant fifteen minutes early. They hugged and immediately started talking.

"You know, you're responsible for the good time I had. I'll always be thankful that you pushed me into going," Kathleen beamed.

"Good. I'm glad. You needed that vacation."

Every moment of her time away had been wonderful, but it was good to be home, too. For the next two hours, Kathleen virtually took her sister on the cruise.

Kathleen looked at her watch. "Now, I have to drop off things at the cleaners, call the attorney to see what's going on with Mom's house, re-bond with Mabel, answer all the emails I avoided on the cruise, and a hundred other things. Can you come over Friday? I'll make a salad and we can talk more."

Lexi beamed a big smile. "Sure. That'll be fun. I'll bring the wine."

Kathleen was having difficulty getting back to a normal routine after her cruise. So many issues were piling up so quickly – church committee meetings, re-scheduling doctor's appointments, returning her passport to the safe deposit box at the bank, and on and on. During the next couple of weeks when she had a break, she worked in her garden. She loved all of the flowers, but her favorite in the backyard was a large red rose bush. It was here that she was working when the phone rang. Quickly, she answered it and sat down on the porch steps. She saw Lexi's name on the phone and gave a cheerful, "Hi."

"Hi, it's me. Have I got news for you, Sis."

"Slow down, Lexi. What's up?"

"I just turned on Facebook and you are the item of the moment. Go turn it on."

Kathleen frowned. "You know better than that, Lexi. I'm not a social media fan. Just tell me what you're talking about."

"Well, you do have Facebook...remember? I put you on a couple of years ago. Just turn it on."

Kathleen knew Lexi was right. She had it, but she'd never used it.

"Okay, calm down. If you're not going to tell me, I'll have to check."

"Enjoy!" and Lexi was off the phone.

Kathleen just shook her head as she walked to the den and her computer. It took her time to figure out how to get Facebook up on the screen. She had forgotten her password and had to search for it.

That accomplished, she started running through conversations of people she didn't even know when suddenly she saw her name. Someone by the name of Tracy had written quite a long message. It was about a woman returning from a ship that had the same name as the one she had sailed on fifty years earlier. And there was more. People were asking Kathleen her name, how old she was, and even one saying, "I knew you fifty years ago, Kathleen. Do you remember?"

Immediately, she clicked off Facebook. "Where has my privacy gone?" Kathleen asked Mabel as she got Lexi on the phone. "Not good Lexi!"

"Oh come on. Keep up with the times. You're not ninety. Don't you think it is exciting to be the star?"

"Definitely not! Facebook makes me nervous. I don't like a mystery, who these people are." Kathleen took a deep breath. "Well, I have things to do. Just wanted to let you know my opinion of the whole thing -- crazy. But thanks for the weird invitation to connect with outer space."

"Alright, but one more thought before you go," Lexi said, keeping her sister on the phone. "What would it be like if someone you hadn't heard from in years turned up on your screen -- an old high school sweetheart for instance?"

Kathleen said in a dry tone, "Good-bye Lexi."

The next day Lexi called back about a phone call she had from her grandson. "Kath, I just heard from Gordon. Thought he was going to surprise us next week, but his plan had not worked out. He wanted to let us know that the annual Fleet Week Celebration begins today in New York and lasts all week. He thought he would be in the city, but he won't be. The navy had other plans for him. Thought it might be something we would enjoy just the same."

"Darn, I wish he could have been here. Funny, I thought of him in Puerto Rico when I saw a navy ship cruising by."

"No, it wasn't him. He's been in California for the last two months."

"How about going on Thursday?" Kathleen asked. "I have an appointment tomorrow. "

"Thursday would be good for me, too. I'll pick you up about eight."

Bright and early two days later, they were off to Manhattan. The waterfront was busy with the Fleet Week Celebration at piers 90 through 92. The navy band could be heard, planes flew overhead saluting the day, banners waved in the wind, and the streets were filled with off duty crews, heading out to visit the city.

Kathleen and Lexi's first stop was aboard a destroyer where the tour lasted half an hour. Kathleen grabbed her sister's arm as they were leaving, "I can't believe that boat is so huge. How can it possibly float?"

"It's big alright, but Gordon told me about an aircraft carrier he was on once. He said they had about 5000 sailors aboard. Can you imagine what it must be like in that kitchen feeding 5,000 people three or more times a day? Now that's gotta be some shopping list. Compare that to your cruise ship."

While walking to the next pier, Kathleen said, "My feet are beginning to ache. Let's find a smaller boat to walk around. There's a submarine here. I was on one in St. Thomas once. They're not as big."

"Let's go."

After walking the length of the sub, stepping over high doorways and along narrow walkways, they climbed out.

"I'm so glad we saw it, but it's not for me," Kathleen said. "Too many people in too small a space for this chicken."

Lexi laughed, and in a more serious tone said, "That's funny. Gosh, I wish Gordon could have been doing all this with us."

*Sorry she missed him being here. I think she's with Gordon in California, not here,* Kathleen thought. *This might distract her for a while. At least I'm going to try.* Kathleen saw an announcement as they were passing the third pier. "Navy ship. Decommissioning ceremony." She drew her sister's attention to the sign.

"Look, Lex. Wonder what that's all about? Let's see what it says. The aircraft carrier has been in mothballs and they're going to decommission it." Kathleen looked at her watch. "The ceremony just began. Do you want to go?"

"Sure. Good idea. I can tell Gordon about it next time we talk, if we can get close enough to hear." The pier was crowded.

On the bow of the ship, representatives of the navy and coast guard were gathered and the program in progress. The speakers were talking about the ship to be decommissioned, its service to the country, and of the captains that served aboard in war and peace. It was suggested to the audience that before they leave to stop by the posters on the dock to see photographs of the captains who had served their country. Kathleen and Lexi tried to move forward, but the crowd was too large, so they gave up.

They didn't know that had they been able to move closer, they would have viewed the last of these captains -- Captain Kevin Johnson.

Lexi dropped Kathleen off at her house. For the next few days, Kathleen continued to work towards her pre-cruise routine. Soon, she and Mabel were back following their comfortable, less hectic activities.

# CHAPTER 15

𝒦athleen's phone rang early one evening while she was responding to emails missed while on her cruise.

"Hello friend. Just had to get in touch. There is no way you are going to be out of my life, you know. I'm anxious for us to get together. Can't do it for the next few days though, I'm busy in the studio."

Kathleen was excited. "Tammy! I'm just so glad you called. You name the time and the place, and I'll be there."

"Let's see how things go here. I'm in and out a lot, but I did want to say hello. Let me call you back in a few days."

"That's fine. I want to hear all about what you're doing."

"It'll be a long lunch," Tammy joked. "Call you later. Bye."

Four days later they met for lunch at Rockefeller Center, happy to be together again. They both ordered Chicken Caesar Salad and a glass of White Zinfandel.

"I'm between shows now, prepping for the next three documentaries," Tammy told Kathleen. "And I want to get down to see my dad in Texas."

"How is he doing?"

"He has been ill for long time as you know. He shouldn't be alone, but my job makes that a problem. And there is no way we can talk him into staying with us here in New York."

"So what are you going to do?"

"My dad comes first. The studio will just have to make the best of it. They can always do re-runs. What have you been up to?"

"My sister and I have been preparing my mother's house for sale and issues of her will. There is a lot to be done."

"I hope that goes smoothly. Wills frighten me. Where there's a will, there's a relative, you know."

They spent an hour together getting caught up and Tammy said she'd be in touch, once her life got organized. Tammy's cell phone interrupted them. "Hold on. Another call." Only seconds later, she returned to Kathleen. "Oops. I've got to be up town in fifteen minutes. See what I mean. This has been great, but I have to leave. I'll call."


Tammy called Kathleen from Texas the following week to tell her the latest news. While she was home, she had called Florence and Joseph, and Lily and Bob. *It was like Tammy to keep in touch,* Kathleen thought as she listened.

"The Davidsons have decided it is time to move to a retirement home." Tammy went on.

"Joseph said it wasn't an easy decision to make, but Florence has not been well and he thought that was where they belonged. The Nesbitt's had been visiting hospitals to see that their hopes and dreams were being fulfilled, and I'm off on another assignment while Michael is playing the author."

They visited for a while, but Tammy had to leave quickly again. She had an appointment. *At the moment,* Kathleen thought, *no exciting news here other than breathing new life into her mother's home and the estate to be taken care of. Maybe I'll write a book one of these days, she thought. Maybe.*

Tammy was still in Texas when she called next.

"Hi, how are things going?" Kathleen was so glad to hear Tammy's voice on the line again. "I've missed you since you went back to Texas. How's your dad? Any better?"

"You know, Kathleen, I'm not sure. His pep has not come back after the latest surgery and it worries me."

"I'm so sorry. It must be difficult for all of you."

"Thank you. That accident really changed his life. Thank God he survived it, but with those scars on his face from his car accident, he is determined he is not going to a retirement place and was not keen on having a caregiver. Just wants to stay here. Away from people."

142

"My mother wanted to stay in her house, too. I think there's comfort for them staying in a familiar environment."

"I want him to do whatever makes him comfortable, but it's difficult with Michael and I working, especially that I have to travel so much. New things always happening at work, too, so it's important that I get back to New York. They've been a little irritated that I've been gone so long. For them, the show's the thing."

"Well, you've been doing what you had to do. I don't want to keep you. Give my regards to Michael and keep that smile on your face. I do hope your dad improves soon."

"Thanks. I'll call when I get back and we can do lunch again."

Meanwhile, the time had come for Kathleen and Lexi to take seriously the restoring their mother's home. It was a lovely old Connecticut house, built in the late twenties. Their parents had bought it long ago and spent their entire lives there. Suburbia was crowding in on them, but they held on. You could still see the rooster weather vane as you came down the street and the apple trees still baring healthy red apples. Kathleen and Lexi loved the house, but they both agreed that they must put it on the market. Lexi's grandson, Gordon, wouldn't be coming back on a permanent basis or they would have offered it to him.

Kathleen and Lexi made arrangements to have it painted and necessary work done on the roof. It would never sell if they hadn't. The interior needed help, too. That was important because they were going to sell the house furnished. They thought it would sell more quickly that way and they had no room for more furniture in either of their homes.

They spent hours choosing fabrics for the living room chairs and couches -- everything was old and faded. They knew a seamstress who would reupholster for less than it would cost to purchase new furniture. The kitchen and bathrooms had been up graded a few years earlier -- their Christmas gift to their mother. Their last Christmas gift. She had held on to so much that was outdated, though. It was a busy time returning the house to a saleable state. They knew there had to be people out there, anxious for a home with the nostalgic charm of the twenties. Now all they had to do was to find them.

## CHAPTER 16

*A*fter a few weeks, Tammy was back in New York. They arranged to meet at the Russian Tea Room.

Kathleen arrived early, anxious to see her friend. Tammy had arranged for a table in a quiet section of the restaurant. *This is prefect since Tammy said she wanted us to spend some time talking.* Within minutes Tammy breezed in. As she always did, she looked like a million dollars.

Kathleen had ordered wine, and they sat back and talked. They were so glad to see each other. It had been almost a month since they had gotten together.

"Well," Tammy said, "what have you been doing since I last talked to you? Don't want you to get in a rut."

"No chance of that right now. Lexi and I have had little free time. We're trying to restore Mother's house. There's a lot to be done before we can put it on the market, but we're getting there, little by little."

Tammy spoke of her dad's health, which she told Kathleen was a great concern to her. Soon, the waiter moved in and they ordered lunch, and then got back to their conversation.

"You said something about being very busy when we last spoke. What's new?" Kathleen asked.

"Well, I have some exciting news to tell you." Tammy was always at her best when she had a story to tell. "When we got back from the cruise, Dad wanted to know all about it. Michael and I spent hours telling him how great the cruise was. It started Dad reminiscing about cruises he had sailed on. He couldn't remember their names, but had no trouble telling us about the good times he had had."

"I can believe that." Kathleen had a sip of wine. "I don't think I was ever on one that I didn't like."

Tammy nodded. "That got him started and we heard about the navy vessels he had been aboard. Those he had no trouble naming. It was so good to see him come out of his shell. One evening we were having a glass of wine before dinner. Suddenly, Dad got up and walked over to the fireplace and leaned his arm on the mantle for support and said, 'I have an idea for you, Tammy. I've been thinking, why don't you see if your show would consider having you do a documentary aboard that ship. If it's as good as you say it is, the powers that be should jump at it.' I told him it was an interesting idea."

"You know, it is. Do you think there's any chance that they might say 'yes'? I can't imagine Kingsley line saying 'no'. The advertising in itself would fill the ship. Call them and see what they say. It can't hurt!"

"Well, I thought he had a good idea, too. I presented my idea -- and believe it or not, everyone said 'yes'!"

Kathleen was so excited for her. She reached across the table and squeezed Tammy's hand. "I just can't believe it, Tammy. What an opportunity that is and a free cruise, too. Can Michael go with you?"

"Not this time, it's business. I had a long conversation with the producer of the show and he's all for it. He thinks that when it's shown it would be a good idea to begin the program by comparing the new ship with the one that sailed fifty years ago."

"That's a great idea."

Tammy held up her hand. "Hold on, Kathleen. In addition to that great idea, he said that he remembered my telling him of a guest who sailed on that first *Noble*."

"I think I might still have some of the original menus and boarding passes I could give you. They could be mounted in some way."

Tammy sat back, raised her glass, and looked knowingly across the table. "Now all I need is someone to interview about *Noble* one."

"You can do it, Tammy. I've certainly told you enough about it."

Tammy now leaned forward in her persuasive way. "Better idea. Why don't you come and help me remember?"

147

"Me? What do you mean?" Kathleen asked, flabbergasted. "I'm not sure I would be up to it. I'm seventy-five. That doesn't draw crowds."

"Kathleen, you're so funny! My feeling is that you may upstage my program. We can talk about the details later. You have to do it!"

Kathleen sat silently, anxiously thinking about the offer. She was torn. *I've never been on TV, but it might be fun. I've got to take care of Mother's house, but maybe it would be okay with Lexi. Life is getting a little more interesting these days*, Kathleen thought. *There's something about Noble cruises. I've been on two and both made changes in my life!!*

Tammy broke into Kathleen's thought. "No option -- your on."

"I guess. Thank you, I think."

With that, lunch was served.

When they had finished dessert, Tammy said, "I have to get back to the studio. They'll be thrilled you agreed."

Kathleen shook her head and smiled. "I did?

Tammy laughed and gave Kathleen one last thought as she got up "I'm leaving this Saturday on *Noble* with my cameraman. We'll get some video on board then be back to interview you. We'll splice it all together."

Kathleen was pre-occupied on her drive back to Connecticut. *Am I really doing this? TV interview? Reliving that first cruise? Life really is changing.*

Tammy sailed and sent Kathleen an email from the cruise ship.

> You're on your way to stardom.
> Buy yourself a jazzy dress and
> we'll knock'm dead. Be ready
> when the camera starts rolling.
> On my return, we will go right
> into production. After the
> shipboard editing is completed,
> we'll talk about your interview.
> I'm so excited. Tammy.

Kathleen was anxious for the next couple of weeks. She made notes, sure she would forget the activities on the first *Noble* ship or the tours that she had taken. *This is okay for now, but what if I don't remember anything when the camera is rolling. What if I blank out? This could be a disaster! How in the heck did I get into this?*

Finally the phone call came. Tammy was back and she told Kathleen she would meet early in the morning with both the director and the story editor of the show.

"Right away? I need to talk to you about what I should say! Your familiar with how this goes, but I'm not."

"That's the whole point. We don't want this done from script. We just want a friendly chat about that first trip. Let it be natural -- fill us in on what that first *Noble* cruise was like. Just don't wear all white, though. It's not good on TV. Did you get a jazzy dress?"

Kathleen Still had questions. "Yes, but what if..."

Tammy interrupted. "Don't worry. I know you'll look fine. Gotta go."

Kathleen didn't sleep that night. *I wonder if I'll remember anything I jotted down,* she thought. I'm a wreck. *I don't even have time to get my hair done! Now what will I do? Wish I had a wig.*

They met at the studio at nine in the morning. Tammy made sure that Kathleen was comfortable and handed her a cup of coffee.

"Oh, that outfit is perfect. You look great." Tammy continued. "Okay, Kathleen, here's what we're doing. First, I will go over there to the set and join the crew, and I will do the basic program. The videographer has put together all of the ingredients to make it a winner. Then we will run the videotape of the cruise to be sure there are no glitches. If there are no problems, we will go on to the second half of the story. That's when you and I will move over to those nice comfortable chairs and we'll just visit. We'll see how it goes. If we're lucky, there will be just one taping."

Kathleen gulped and then settled back. This was her first experience at watching a show being taped. There were technicians, the producer, stage

manager, cameramen, and even makeup people and a
hairdresser.

She thought, b*et Tammy's easy going manner and
humor will make viewers want to sign up for a cruise.* Kathleen
was so lost in watching all the preparations that she
almost forgot what was coming next, until the makeup
artist and the hairdresser approached her. They spent
fifteen minutes doing touch-ups before Kathleen was
to be taped.

*Tammy hadn't told me about this, but I can get used to it
very quickly. I wonder if there are any other surprises in store for
me?*

Tammy returned from the set. Now it's time for
you and I to visit the first *Noble*. She laughed as she
saw her friend being fussed over. "It's a piece of cake,
Kathleen."

Kathleen hoped so!

Bright lights were on the two lounge chairs for
Kathleen and Tammy. They moved over to the small
set and sat in chairs facing each other. Kathleen's heart
began to pound -- her palms were damp. Tammy saw
her anxiety and knew she had to put her at ease.

"Well," she said, looking directly at Kathleen,
"What luck it was that you and I were at the same table
on the new *Noble* ship. I would never have known a
darn thing about the first *Noble* cruise fifty years ago,
otherwise. Did you really think there was a big
difference?"

That did the trick and Kathleen almost forgot where she was and what she was doing. She was off and running. The conversation became spontaneous. Tammy knew it was exactly what the producer wanted -- it was a winner.

When the interview was over, Tammy asked Kathleen to wait just a few minutes while she and the producer went to the screening room to see what they had. Within a half hour, Tammy was back.

"It's a go. The producer is satisfied, the director is satisfied, the videographer is satisfied, and I'm satisfied. You're really did a great job, Kathleen. Their job now is to put all the pieces together. Let's go and have something to eat."

The show date had been decided and Tammy took off for Texas until then. She wanted to get back to her dad. Kathleen once again was able to get a good night sleep. *That wasn't hard. Just talked about what I know. I'm so happy she didn't ask about my romance. My only worry.* The next day she was off to work on the finishing touches of her mother's house. Lexi had done so much and Kathleen wanted to do her share now.

# CHAPTER 17

Tammy and Michael returned to Texas. She found her dad about the same. When he retired from the navy, life had been great even though he had to pace himself after the heart attack. This was a very different life than he had as captain on an aircraft carrier. He played golf, fished, and even taught a Sunday school class. He was a happy man. Then it happened.

He was driving back from a great weekend reunion with some of his navy buddies. There was a head-on crash. His survival was questionable for a long time. He made it through, but not without permanent scars. There had been a fire upon impact and it took time to get him out of his crushed vehicle. There were months of plastic surgery. Some operations were successful and some left serious scars, especially on his face. It changed his looks and changed his life.

During this period Tammy had been commuting back and forth. Now she was glad to be back in Texas with him for a while. She was tireless in trying to keep his spirits up.

One night at dinner, Tammy told her dad and Michael that she had a surprise for them. She didn't want to tell them about it until after the special dinner she had prepared.

"Okay, now into the living room for the big event, guys."

Tammy put a bowl of popcorn next to her dad's chair, turned down the lights, and turned on the TV. Within minutes they were on board *Noble* II, watching her latest documentary, commercials and all. Tammy moderated as only Tammy could – interrupting the program from time to time to offer highlights. Pointing to the screen, she said, "That's a very special woman. She and I spent a lot of time together. Kathleen is seventy-five and used to be a travel agent. It's amazing how much she knows about the Carribean. We had a great time especially in St. Thomas. Went shopping together. Oh, right there! That's where I bought the necklace with the red shell."

"Okay. Okay, Tammy. Let's see the rest of your interview," Michael said.

Tammy spoke faster. "I will, but just quickly, she's the best guest I ever had on my show. Kind. A lovely woman."

Michael and her Dad were quiet as the fifty-year history of Kingsley Cruise Lines was spun. When the show ended, Michael turned and asked Tammy's father, "Well, what did you think of that daughter of yours?"

"What did I ever think of her? Your wife is a master at her profession. It was all wonderful." He stopped, slowly reached for a handful of popcorn, and quietly said, "And that addition of, uh, interviewing your friend who was on the first ship…" He stopped again, clearing his throat, "… just added a special twist."

"And it was nice to have the narrator right in the room with us providing brief moments of interruption," Michael teased.

Tammy was happy. "It was your idea, Dad. I just followed through with it. Thanks," Tammy said and gave her father a kiss. The evening ended on a happy note.

## CHAPTER 18

$\mathcal{T}$ammy had to get back to New York. She had promised the crew and staff of the station a party to celebrate the show. She called Kathleen.

"Hi, Kathleen. I'm still in Texas, but wanted to call you. Hope you have recovered from that TV ordeal."

"Oh, I think I'll be alright. Just waiting for Spielberg to call," Kathleen joked.

"That's always possible. Just let him know I'm available too. We have a wrap party after we finish each show. Save next Saturday. There are cocktails at four at our apartment. I'll email you my address. You've got to come to the party. My whole crew will be there. You're the star."

Kathleen was delighted that Tammy was coming back to New York and promised to be there.

Most of the production company had arrive before Kathleen. A phone call from the family lawyer with regard to her mother's estate had held her up.

"Phew. Am I glad to see you," Tammy greeted her. "I thought the honored guest had deserted us.

"Kathleen explained why she was late and went in to meet everyone. It was a lovely party. Everyone had nice things to say to her about her part in Tammy's program. Kathleen was so pleased with all the nice things everyone had to say and was excited to meet everyone again in this more relaxing environment than the studio.

"Now," Tammy said, "I have someone I'd like you to meet." She took Kathleen's arm and they walked across the living room to where her father sat in a quiet corner. "Surprise! My dad is here and I want you to meet him. It wasn't easy to get him to come, but I managed and I think you will be good for him. You two are about the same age, so I think he will be relaxed talking with you."

"Great," Kathleen said. "You've talked about him so often, I almost feel as though I know him."

Tammy's father was sitting in a chair away from the group. He had asked his daughter if he might sit quietly at the party, self-conscious about his disfigurement.

"Dad, this is my friend and theatrical partner, Kathleen. The star of my latest program."

Kathleen smiled.

"Tammy didn't tell me that you would be here tonight. I'm so glad you are." He rose and there was a smile on his face as they shook hands. Kathleen sat in a chair next to him.

"I can't tell you how happy I am to meet you," Kathleen said. "It's almost like visiting an old friend. Tammy speaks of you so often that I feel that I know you. You're a very important person to that girl of yours! If I had had a daughter, I would want her to be just like Tammy."

"That's nice to hear," he said, sitting back down.
"I almost feel that we are old friends, too. Ever since
she returned from her cruise, she has spoken of you.
That must have been a great time at the captain's
table."

"It really was," Kathleen agreed.

"I even know about the table that was set up in
your honor and the wild night at the casino."

Kathleen laughed. "We really had so much fun."

Tammy had left them to chat. She was the hostess
and there were things to be done.

"By the way, Kathleen," her father continued still
smiling, "I saw you on TV the other night. You have a
great memory. I was impressed. You really brought
that first *Noble* to life. It must have been a great
experience for you. Tammy said you were reasonably
young when you went."

"Yes, I was in my twenties. Hard to believe I was
ever that young." Kevin leaned over and patted her
hand softly. She went on. "I was really anxious about
doing the show, afraid that I wouldn't remember
things with the camera on me, but Tammy insisted.
Actually, once that daughter of yours did her magic --
made me forget where I was -- it became a lot of fun! I
have lots of memories of that cruise, it was a special
time in my life and I loved talking about it."

Kevin smiled. "That's one of the nice things
about age, we have memories to fall back on."

Kathleen nodded and agreed.

Soon, their conversation turned to Tammy and her many talents. He obviously was proud of his daughter.

"Now, tell me something about yourself, Kathleen."

"There is not a great deal to tell. I spent most of my life in travel. For many years I was an agent and eventually bought the agency. I did lots of traveling. It's been a good life."

When Tammy returned, her father and Tammy were knee-deep in conversation, forgetting about the party just across the living room.

"Well, you two seem to have no trouble getting to know each other. I was watching you and you were gabbing away full speed. I'm so glad you met. You're two of my favorite people." Tammy tapped her father on the shoulder. "All right, Dad. You know I always keep my promises. Three hours. Times up. If you will excuse him, Kathleen, I promised his doctor that I wouldn't let him overdue."

Her dad shook his head and stood up. "She's the boss." He turned to Kathleen, smiled, and shook both of her hands, holding them for a long moment, looking directly into her eyes. "Tonight has been special for me. Thank you for our visit." Tammy took her father's arm and they moved down the hall to his bedroom.

Kathleen stayed for another hour then made her apologies and left for her long ride home back to

Connecticut. Michael walked with her downstairs and saw her to her car.

## CHAPTER 19

*I*t had been a lovely evening for Kathleen. Tammy's friendship had made Kathleen's life more interesting in so many ways she thought as she drove home.

The next few days were busy again. She and Lexi were trying to wrap-up things left undone in their mother's house. They wanted to get it ready for sale so their lives could get back to normal.

Then late one night Kathleen had a call from Tammy. Her dad had had a setback.

"He's in Presbyterian Hospital. As soon as he can be moved, we'll take him home," Tammy said.

"What happened? What can I do, Tammy?"

"He had another heart attack. He's in intensive care. There's nothing to do right now, but wait. I'll call you in a day or two."

Kathleen knew what Tammy must be going through since her mother had had a heart attack just a few months earlier. She had not realized, however, how serious Tammy's father's health issues were. A couple of days later she heard from Tammy again.

"Sorry not to have called sooner, but we have been at the hospital night and day. Michael and I had a little rest last night, here at our apartment. Dad's heart has not been good for a long time, but we had no idea how bad. They've had him in ICU and only today he was transferred to a private room."

"Why, that sounds good."

"It is. The doctor says he thinks if we are careful, he can make the trip home. More tests today and if things look good, I'll take him back to Texas where his regular cardiologist is. If you would like to run in and say 'hi,' I think it might pep him up. He spoke of the nice visit he had with you."

"I'd like that. I'd like to visit him today, if he is leaving soon. Where do I go?"

Tammy gave her directions and they decided that the best time would be during afternoon visiting hours.

"We're going back to the hospital in a half hour, forty-five minutes. There's a large waiting room on the first floor. Let's meet there and I'll take you up to his room."

"Fine, see you as soon as I can get to the city. Oh, by the way if I get there early is it alright if I go to his room? You know what traffic is like getting into the city. Would you believe, I don't know your dad's name…."

Tammy cut her off in mid sentence. "Whoops, the phone. I've got another call. It's the doctor. I'll see you soon." And she was gone.

Kathleen arrived early. Just as she pulled up at the entrance, she saw Tammy getting out of a cab. The timing couldn't have been better. They took the elevator to Kevin's floor. Tammy suggested that Kathleen wait while she got approval for her to visit. Tammy showed her to a waiting room while she made the arrangements.

She came back soon, but not with good news. The orders had said no visitors other than immediate family.

"I'm so sorry, Kathleen. I should have checked first. I'm just not thinking straight right now. I know he would have enjoyed seeing you. I wish you didn't have that drive back to Connecticut. Do you want to stay at my place tonight?" Tammy asked.

"No, I think I'll go right on home. Thanks though. Don't worry about it. The only thing important is to get your dad back on his feet. If quiet is what he needs, then that's what he must have. When you get to Texas give me a call. And tell your dad that he is in my prayers. I really enjoyed our visit the other night."

They hugged and Tammy walked down the hall to her dad's room.

Kathleen tried to get her on the phone a couple of days later but with no luck. She left a message.

Tammy called back the next week. They spoke briefly.

"Should have called you sooner, but Dad's care has taken a lot of time. Michael and I take turns. He likes having us around."

"How do you think things are going, Tammy? Does he seem to be improving?"

"You know Kathleen, I just don't know. He stays in bed now and spends his waking time just writing pages and pages on a yellow pad. Maybe he is writing his autobiography. I didn't ask. He just writes and writes. Well, it keeps him busy, but it is so unlike him. I think I'll stay in Texas. He needs me, -- and I need him."

Kathleen didn't interrupt. She just let Tammy talk. She knew how hard all of this was for her and she needed to get things out.

Only three days later, it was over. Tammy called to say that her dad passed away peacefully in his sleep.


Kathleen heard from her a couple of weeks later.

"Hi. It's me again. Dad's death has sort of thrown me for a loop. I don't know what to do. Now we have learned that Michael has to go to Michigan. Someone is interested in his book. Considering using it in some college courses. I'm not crazy about being left alone here right now."

"Of course your not. I'll leave as soon as I can get a ticket," Kathleen said.

"I knew it. There aren't many friends that would do that. Thanks, Kathleen. Just text me what time your plane arrives. I'm so glad you are coming."

"Me, too."

# CHAPTER 20

$K$athleen was at the airport early. When she booked the flight the night before, she was told that it was the last seat still available. They were right. The plane was full. Her seat was half way back and next to a large man who had the aisle seat. He seemed annoyed when she had to ask him to move while she got to her seat in the middle.

Soon a flight attendant walked down the aisle making sure all seatbelts were fastened. As she passed their row, Kathleen's seatmate looked up from his paper.

"Are we gonna get a free meal on this plane?"

"Not any more," the flight attendant replied. "Those days are gone forever. You can purchase them though. There is a menu in the pocket in front of you. Can I get you some coffee after we are airborne?"

"No, I'll wait," he growled and turned to Kathleen with a shrug. "They'll be charging for oxygen next."

Not wanting to get into a discussion about the airline industry, Kathleen merely said, "Guess we have to expect charges in this economy."

"Yeah, guess so," he grumbled and settled back to read his "Wall Street Journal."

Before long, the flight attendant came over the speaker advising the passengers of the emergency procedures.

"What next?" the man along side of Kathleen asked, obviously not happy. "All I want to do is finish my paper."

Kathleen was tempted to reply, but thought better of it.

They arrived in Dallas right on time and Tammy was there and waiting. After picking up the luggage, they were off. "It is about an hour's drive," she said. It gave them time to talk.

Kathleen noticed that Tammy really needed that. She began to relax a little as she drove Kathleen through the lovely countryside. The drive was easy, no traffic to speak of. About forty-five minutes from the airport, Tammy turned off the highway and drove through a small town. Kathleen noticed that she slowed down as they went along.

"This is where I grew up. I wanted you to see it. You know, we all move around a lot these days. Changed addresses a good deal, but I think everyone has one special place that they call home. This is home to me."

As they drove along she pointed out her high school, the house where she had grown up, a small library, and the church where she had gone to Sunday school. It was a temporary reprieve from the sadness that she had been feeling. Her old smile was back.

Kathleen looked out the car window. "I think hometowns are forever in our minds. You never forget them, do you?"

"Never."

They drove on and soon Tammy turned onto a long driveway that led to a lovely white colonial house standing high on a rolling green hilltop. There were large old trees and colorful flowers everywhere. It looked so peaceful and so pretty.

Tammy parked in the circular driveway, got out, grabbed Kathleen's luggage, and preceded Kathleen up the fieldstone walk. At the door she turned to make sure Kathleen had no problem and lead the way into a large foyer. The room's soft light came from a glass globe hanging from the center of the ceiling. She dropped the bags on the tiled floor and suggested to Kathleen that she throw her jacket over the nearby bench. No welcome mat was needed when you entered this house.

Tammy took Kathleen's arm. "Come on, let me show you where I live." It all was so Tammy.

The living room walls were creamy white and the tall round-topped windows held crisp yellow linen drapes that hung to the floor. Two deep-seated grey couches, slightly slanted toward a large stone fireplace. On the mantle was a Seth Thomas clock and framed pictures of Tammy's family. A low mahogany antique table stood in front of the couches, allowing room for a morning cup of coffee or a glass of wine. The chairs looked comfy and were casually placed around the room.

"Tammy," Kathleen asked, looking across the room at a large oil painting on the far wall, "that oil painting surely looks like the house you just showed me -- where you grew up. Is that why you chose it?"

"No, as a matter of fact it was Dad's. His mother painted it a few years before her death. When we moved in here, he gave it to me. He said he didn't want me to forget where I came from. Roots were important to him."

"It's a beautiful painting. You're so lucky to have it."

Tammy smiled, she knew how much that painting meant to her father -- and to her.

Moving across the room, Kathleen stopped to smell a large bowl of mixed cut flowers. "From your garden, I'll bet."

"They are. That's one of the reasons I like to get down here. I love to garden and Central Park takes a dim view to me arriving with my gardening equipment. Down here, I have a man that comes in twice a week to take care of the grounds when I'm back east.

"Oh, come on. I'll bet you could get away with gardening in Central Park. Bring your photographer." Tammy laughed.

Kathleen continued looking around. The only thing missing, she thought, was a plaque she had recently seen in Bloomingdales – "Stay awhile. Relax. The wine is cooling." It would be perfect here.

Tammy was anxious to get dinner going. She slid her arm through Kathleen's and they moved on to the kitchen. "Are you as hungry as I am?"

"I have to admit I am."

Kathleen was impressed with Tammy's decorating skills again. The walls were the palest blue – almost white, glass in the cabinets displayed her blue and white china, and the white Carrera marble counters captured a swirl of pale blue. Blue and white checked curtains at the window set the tone. Obviously, Tammy loved blue.

Tammy walked over and opened the French doors. Sunshine and flowers everywhere -- picture perfect. They could even hear birds in the garden.

Sitting on a tall stool at the counter, Kathleen sighed, "I just can't get over what a lovely home you have."

Tammy smiled and poured them a glass of wine. Earlier, she had made a shrimp salad. She heated rolls and then refilled the wine glasses. She brought everything to the counter and sat down on a stool next to Kathleen. It was catch-up time.

When they had finished their salad, Tammy suggested that they have dessert later and take their coffee into the den. "You haven't seen the cruise tape," Tammy noted. "Let's go in the other room and

I'll turn on the tape." They both settled back into soft leather chairs as Tammy's program began.

"Great, I've been so anxious to see it."

They watched and enjoyed it all, making occasional remarks and sometimes laughing at themselves.

"Not bad, was it?" Tammy quipped.

"I think you'd better count your blessing that it all went well this time, having an amateur interviewed," Kathleen laughed.

"No question. I knew it would."

Tammy ran it again and they joked about Kathleen's anxiety that day. "I'll never forget the look on your face when the makeup artist came in."

"It never entered my head that I was going to be transformed!"

Tammy shifted in her chair so she could look right at Kathleen. "Now, I have another surprise for you."

"Tammy, you've been surprising me ever since we meet."

"Lets see how you feel about this one. But first, how about that desert?"

"Do you really think I can eat anything when one of your surprises is in the air?"

"Alright. I had a phone call from my studio yesterday. We actually pleased those New York pros. My boss said that the program had the largest viewer rating that they ever had. We did it!"

171

"Wow -- that's wonderful. Did you expect that sort of report?"

"Nope. I thought the show would be successful, but his remarks exceeded my expectation. But that's not all. The powers that be put their heads together and a new show is in the works."

"Don't stop there. What do they have in mind for you now --checking outer space?"

"That's a thought, but right now the show has more of a mother-daughter theme. They are trying to come up with something where you and I can do monthly trips -- show what makes a successful merger of the two ages as they travel." Tammy sighed. "Oh, I don't know what it's all about. They're full of ideas and nothing will happen immediately. It never does. Let's let it go for now. Just something to think about."

And Kathleen did. *This was scary stuff. It isn't just a one-night show – it's big business.*

Tammy walked back to the kitchen, giving Kathleen time to sort out the news. From the kitchen she called, "Whipped cream on your pie?"

"I hate to disappoint you, but no thanks. Let's just have another cup of coffee."

By ten o clock they were both tired and talked out and soon were off to bed.

## CHAPTER 21

𝒦athleen woke early the next morning. Her room filled with bright sunshine, which seemed to be usual here. She pulled on her robe and walked over to the window and could hardly believe how lovely the view was. The back yard was one huge garden. Yellow daffodils, red cannas, lilies, and lilac bushes everywhere. Weeping willow trees gracefully lowered their branches as the soft breezes filled the yard. Birds were chatting on the branches. For a few moments she just stood and listened. It was such a good sound and such a beautiful sight.

Kathleen's attention soon was drawn by strange sounds coming from downstairs. She quickly threw on clothes and went to investigate. Following the sound into the kitchen, Kathleen could hardly believe what she saw. Six little Shih Tzus were running around and pouncing on each other. She was fascinated. Tammy was busy putting food in their bowls. Kathleen just stood by and watched as they ran over to their dishes. Tails wagged like mad while they ate.

"Good morning. You never told me you had puppies. Oh my gosh, they're so cute," Kathleen said.

Tammy turned. "Good morning to you, too. Aren't they special? I only wish they were mine. Actually they belong to my neighbor. Her son is graduating from college and I offered to keep them while she was gone. It's going to be hard to let them go."

Their meal finished, the puppies ran across the room and scrambled to get up on Kathleen's lap. She picked one up and it snuggled right into her neck. It reminded her of Mabel.

"That's Olivia," Tammy pointed out.

"She's the snuggler." Tammy gave Kathleen time to enjoy them then took six leashes off a hook on the wall. When the dogs saw the leashes, they made a dash to sit in front of Tammy.

"Okay, guys, its time to go out."

They sat while she leaned down and hooked the leashes in their collars. Once on, they twisted and turned, anxious to get going.

"Kathleen, you can walk with me, or you might like to take a cup of coffee outside and sit in the patio until I get back."

"I can't resist that cup of coffee. You go on. I'll pour it and go on outside."

The six puppies dashed to the door.

Kathleen thought to herself as she gazed at Tammy gardens, *why would anyone want an apartment in a city when they have this. I'd retire. I'm sure she can afford it!*

She sat back and enjoyed her coffee and the warm breeze. Before long, she heard the scratch of little feet on the driveway. When they were close to the house,

Tammy undid the dogs' leashes and they all rushed up to the patio.

"Aren't you worried about them running away?"

"Just wait and you'll see why I'm not." Tammy walked over to a box
on the table and took out six little squares. "Alright girls, look what I have."

She opened the back door and stood in the entrance. "Treat time. Treat time," she called out. With that the puppies made a wild dash into the house. "Mission accomplished." Tammy closed the door behind them and joined Kathleen.

"Tammy, this is the life."

"That's true, but you have to be away for awhile before you really appreciate it. Dad loved it out here on the patio. We used to sit here and have long talks."

She turned, went inside, then returned with the first breakfast tray. It had a small vase with a daisy in the center. There were blueberry waffles, a pitcher of warm syrup, sausage, orange juice and a pot of coffee. She presented it to Kathleen and returned with a second tray for herself.

"This looks so good! Your spoiling me, but I must admit, I love it," Kathleen told her hostess.

## CHAPTER 22

*T*ammy sighed as she poured them a second cup of coffee. "You know, Kathleen, I've had lots of time to think lately. I thought that I had reached the pinnacle of the good life. Only now am I beginning to realize that it's not always about things. Both of my parents are gone and I wonder if they ever really knew how I felt about them, or was I too busy to show them." Tears filled her eyes.

She could see how troubled Tammy was. Kathleen put her coffee cup on her tray. "Tammy, you've told me many times about the good times you had with both of them. Come on, remember those and pull them out every once in awhile. Think about those good times. They loved you and they knew that you loved them --you were a good daughter, Tammy."

She leaned over and grabbed Kathleen's hand. This was just what she needed. She pulled herself together and said, "Thanks, Kathleen. Now let's get these dirty dishes in the house and then go shopping. There's nothing like shopping to perk me up."

The next few days were busy. They shopped, went sightseeing, saw a good movie, and then ate -- a lot. On the last day of Kathleen's stay, Tammy had some calls to make to New York. Kathleen went outside to enjoy her book. She loved that patio and, sitting there, thought about how nice this must have been for Tammy's dad. *He apparently needed privacy and the surroundings were so peaceful and so beautiful, he had to find comfort here.*

Suddenly the kitchen door flew open and Tammy hurried out. "Kathleen, guess what? Dad asked me to give you this when I saw you." She handed her an envelope. "It's probably a thank you for your kindness to him at the apartment. I had taken it out of his room and laid it on my desk and forgot about it. Just found it when I went in the den to make my calls."

"How nice of him. Will you lay it on the table and I'll get to it in a few minutes. I have about four or five pages left and I still don't know who done it."

"Sure." Tammy laid the envelope down. "I found a large manila envelope under his bed addressed to me. I looked inside and saw that yellow pad he had been working on -- just haven't had the courage to pull it out and read it yet. I will, though. He often commented on family genealogy. I think maybe that's what it is. Get back to your reading. I have a few more calls to make."

She went inside and Kathleen continued reading. After about ten minutes, she finished her book and slapped it down on the table. She always hated finishing books, especially when they were as good as this one was.

*Now let's see what Tammy's dad had to say. It was nice of him to remember me.* She picked up the envelope and walked out along the garden path. She had been sitting all morning and thought it would be a good idea to move around. She knew there were benches around the nearby small lake and decided to walk up there. Texas had turned warm. She walked around the lake where shade from the large trees would keep her cool. Kathleen found a good spot to sit and read. She opened the envelope and pulled out two pages of yellow lined paper. *What in the world? Two pages?*

> Dear Kathleen. First let me tell you what a treat it was to spend time with you at Tammy's party. It was so nice to see what good friends you and Tammy have become. Now Kathleen, I have a confession to make. One that I only hope you will understand. You won't without an explanation, though. I'll do my best and how I hope it will all make sense.

Kathleen was confused. *Why an explanation? What about? Maybe he was talking about his face.* Tammy had said that really bothered him. She read on.

> Kathleen, it's a long story that I have to tell you and who knows, maybe I won't have time to finish it, but I'll try. I know that time is short. My accident has made it impossible for me to be the man I once was. I am sure Tammy told you about it.

*This gets stranger and stranger*, Kathleen thought and read on.

> Before coming to New York, Tammy showed
> Michael and I the completed TV show you and
> she did. I quietly watched it all, but during that
> hour my world fell apart when I saw you.
> Kathleen -- I'm Kevin.

Kathleen chocked back a sob, "Oh, God, no! It's a joke. I would have known him!" She flung the letter to the ground. *Please God; make it not be true,* she pleaded. *Maybe I missed something.* She leaned over and hurriedly picked up the pages in her trembling hands, trying to read them again through her tears.

Kevin went on about the letter he had put under the door and the search he had made when the ship lost the contact information she had given the purser office.

> I will spend the rest of my life wondering why
> you and I never discussed addresses and telephone
> numbers. But then, we never expected that terrible
> change of events. I checked travel agencies in
> phone books looking for you. There were several
> Kathleen O'Connell's, but never you. Fifty years
> have gone by, Kathleen, but I have never forgotten
> those days in St. Thomas. I have carried that red
> shell all these years. And, do you remember the
> 1812 Hotel and how time stood still? I do. You know,
> addresses and names seemed to change the course

of our lives. When Tammy spoke of us, I was always "dad" and you were unnamed - just "my friend". She didn't know. If only she had.

"Oh, my God," Kathleen sobbed. "This is like a crazy dream. It can't end like this!" She brushed away her tears and read on.

Before I finish I want you to know I have never loved again and I can only believe we still haven't finished our dream. Where, I don't know, but what I do know is that it's not over. It never will be. I love you, Kathleen.     Kevin

She just couldn't believe what she read. As she sat there, torrents of tears streamed down her face. Devastated, she couldn't move.

Tammy finished her phone calls and went out on the patio with two glasses of iced coffee and two photo albums. This was Kathleen's last day and Tammy wanted her to see photos of her dad before he had his accident. Expecting to see Kathleen relaxing on a lounge chair, she was surprised not to find her there. She put the albums and the coffee down on the patio table and looked out at the garden. She wasn't there.

Tammy became concerned as time went on that Kathleen hadn't come back. She checked the house to see if her friend had gone upstairs to pack. She wasn't there, either. The sun was going down and if Kathleen had gone for a walk, Tammy thought she might have difficulty finding her way back. She doubted that Kathleen would go up to the lake, but it was the only place left to look. Tammy hurried up the path. Now she was worried. The last time she had seen her was when she had given her the envelope from her dad. What a relief it was when she got to the lake and saw Kathleen sitting on a bench at the far end.

The sound of Tammy's footsteps on the fallen leaves alerted Kathleen who quickly wiped her eyes, trying to camouflage her emotions.

"For crying out loud, what are you doing sitting up here?" Tammy called out as she circled the lake. Approaching Kathleen, she said, "It's getting close to dark and I have to confess, I thought you might have run off with a traveling salesman."

Kathleen looked up and gave her a brief smile.

"You're a mess, Kathleen. Your face is so red. You have to be careful out in the sun. You're fair skinned and you don't need a sunburn!"

Kathleen had folded the letter and put it in her pant's pocket when she saw Tammy coming toward her. "Is it really red? I just needed to walk around a little and I guess I didn't think about the sun."

"Okay, well, the party's over. Come on back to the house and we'll make a lady of you." With that, they slowly walked back down the hill.

## CHAPTER 23

Once inside, Tammy in her usual direct way said, "You got a lot of sun today and your hair is a mess. Why don't you fix yourself up? Relax for a while."

"Maybe I should. I am a little tired."

"I think a nice omelet and a good strong cup up coffee will do the trick. Maybe a Mimosa? I'll have everything ready when you come on down."

Kathleen climbed the stairs, too numb to even think. All she wanted to do was to crawl into bed, but she didn't. She dabbed her face with a washcloth, put on a caftan, and twenty minutes later she went back downstairs.

Kathleen joined Tammy in the kitchen. "Well, that sure made a difference."

Tammy turned. "You really had me scared for a minute. Sit down and I'll bring our omelets to the kitchen table."

Kathleen made it through dinner. *I can't tell her right now,* she thought. *What good would it do? She doesn't need anything else on her mind. Losing her dad was enough.*

After dinner, Tammy suggested that they just put the dishes in the sink. She would get to them later. "Come on. I have something to show you. Let's go in the family room and get comfy."

Kathleen had come to help her through a tough period and she was not going to spoil it. With unbelievable effort, she set her heartache aside for a little while. Tammy sat down on the couch beside her with an album.

"Okay, well here we go. I thought you might like to see a few pictures of Dad and I."

Slowly Tammy turned the pages. There were lots of pictures. Pictures of Tammy as a child, in crutches after the bicycle accident when she broke her leg, time at college, Tammy the bride, and recent pictures of Tammy.

"All right," she flattened her hand on the book. "Here's what I really want you to see." Showing it was something she had planned. With that, she flipped to the next page and there he was.

Tammy continued. "If you saw him before the accident, you probably would not recognize him now, but this is my dad before the accident. Wasn't he handsome!"

Kathleen's heart stopped for a moment then started pounding deep in her chest. She couldn't move. She couldn't utter a word. There he was, young as she had known him. Her eyes dampened.

Tammy turned to Kathleen to see her reaction.

Kathleen pulled herself together and wiped away a few tears. "I think you were one lucky girl. I can feel your heartache at losing your handsome dad."

"Yes, he was that kind of a man. Kind and gentle. Everyone that knew him loved him. I am so glad that you two had those moments in my apartment at the party to be together and visit."

Kathleen smiled and Tammy went on to show her more pictures. In a little while Tammy said, "I'm keeping you up and I know you need some sleep. I did want you to see those pictures of dad, though. You're plane doesn't leave until late afternoon tomorrow, so go up and get a good nights sleep. Let's get up early and go out for breakfast. I know a little restaurant with the worlds best breakfast quiche!"

"You're right. I'm tired, but I'll be up early. That quiche sounds too good to miss. Thank you so much for showing me the pictures, tonight."

## CHAPTER 24

𝒦athleen's night was the longest in her life. She went over and over the letter in her mind. It drove her almost mad. She asked herself questions that had no answers. *What would have happened if we had stayed on the deck all night? If I hadn't continued to use my single name at the agency? If I hadn't used my stupid nickname, Lena? Would he have found me? If. If. If. My life is a result of If's.*

Her memories were all over the place and eventually went back to the first time she and Kevin met. She remembered it so clearly – like a movie re-run. It was a chilly morning. Kathleen had come out on deck early, chosen a deck chair, and laid back, wrapping herself in the blanket that had been provided. It was chilly. She snuggled down and soon drifted off to sleep. A bump on her chair woke her. Looking up, she saw a handsome redheaded man with a wonderful smile looking down at her. It was Kevin. He claimed she was snoring as he walked by. Kathleen could still hear that little tease in his voice when he said, "I just want to be sure you were all right." She could have been indignant -- but she wasn't. She remembered laughing.

It began that way. Their first real day together. They were both young and single. She was a widow and he had gone through a recent divorce. They enjoyed everything the ship had to offer -- together.

They were in St Thomas four days. Two were on the itinerary and two because of some problem with the ship's engines that kept them in port. She thought to herself there was no way she would ever forget those days. They were bitter-sweet memories.

Through the night she went over and over things. They were all so fresh. It could have been yesterday. More than anything else, she remembered their time at the beach. About them swimming through the pounding surf. Kathleen could almost feel the salty spray as they walked along the shoreline, searching for sea glass and shells.

The memory of the red shell with the tiny white dots laying there on the white sand was vivid. Tears filled her eyes as she remembered that moment when she scooped up the shell and handed it to him, saying, "Here's something for you to remember me by." Those eight words changed the course of their relationship. She could feel him put out his hand and pull her close, wrapping his arms around her and holding her tightly. he gave her that first kiss – gently.

She didn't stop. She couldn't. She had gone over those moments and there were no answers. *Why was there no "good-bye?" If he loved me so much*, she asked herself, *why would he walk off the ship without seeing me? Couldn't he at least knock on my door before he left?*

Those two days changed their lives. It all ended too quickly when he left the ship early to rush to his young daughter who had been hit by a car. It was Tammy. She found little relief as she went over and over those days, realizing there was nothing she could do about it. He was gone.

Early the next morning Kathleen dragged herself out of bed and took her shower. She had some last minute packing to do. Before going down stairs, she put a wet cloth on her face -- the puffiness under her swollen eyes was a dead giveaway to her crying. She just hoped Tammy wouldn't notice.

## CHAPTER 25

*I*t was so quiet when she walked into the den. Tammy was out walking the dogs. The album that they had looked at the night before was still on the coffee table. *I need one more look,* she said to herself as she began to turn the pages. Suddenly, she heard the sound of the puppies. Quickly she closed the album and hurried into the kitchen.

Tammy was in a cheerful mood. "You're up and ready for breakfast. Let's get going early. It's a very popular spot. First, though, I have to feed the puppies and get them out once more."

Soon they were off to town. It was a beautiful August morning, though cool for Texas. They drove along quiet country roads, keeping away from the highway. Tammy wanted to show Kathleen how pretty this part of Texas was. When they reached the restaurant, Tammy pulled into a space right in front.

"We're lucky, Kathleen. Gentle Breezes is one of the most popular restaurants in the area. A couple of hours later, chances are we would have to park a good distance away."

Tammy loved the area and the restaurant especially. She wanted to share it with her friend. Large pots with purple and yellow pansies rimed the curved flagstone path attached to the low, sprawling restaurant was a large patio with purple and yellow umbrellas covering large, round tables. Kathleen could see them through the white picket fence as they drove up. Containers with bright flowering plants were everywhere. She thought again, *what a lovely place this area is to live in.*

They had the breakfast special and the quiche lived up to Tammy's recommendation.

Kathleen asked, "Did you ever think of writing a travel book about this part of Texas, Tammy? Or are you trying to keep it a secret? Of course, it might lose its charm if it became too popular."

"Correct! Long waiting lines are not what this is about. This is our village and we want to keep it this way," Tammy proudly said.

"Your right. I've heard that before. You can't blame tourists for looking for something they will always remember, but I hear that people living in the midst of a resort area yearn for the season to be over. They want their peaceful life restored."

"That's it exactly. You've got that right. Nice thing is, here there's no pressure to eat and move on. Their motto is, 'have another cup of coffee and relax'."

Kathleen agreed, though still reeling from last night's revelation, made relaxing not easy for her to do.

They talked about Tammy's return to the city and Kathleen spoke of the work that she and Lexi had done on her mother's house. Both stayed away, for a time, from their mutual heartaches.

189

"All right, Kathleen, where do we go from here?" Tammy asked as they walked back to the car. "We have a few hours before you leave and the choice is yours -- shopping or sightseeing, or we can go back to the house if you would rather."

"You mentioned that there had been a memorial service. I have been wondering where he is buried. If it is not too upsetting for you, could we run out to the cemetery?"

Tammy seemed to hold her breath for a minute. This was something that she knew she must share with Kathleen that she kept putting off.

"That can't be done, Kathleen. Dad had written out his wishes and I followed through with them. Like so many that had spent a good part of their lives in the navy, he wanted to be cremated and to be buried at sea. I am waiting to hear from the navy what I am to do. They'll inform me of course as to the time and place that I am to send Dad's ashes. They will go aboard a navy ship leaving port. That's what Dad wanted."

Telling Kathleen that her father was not being buried was so hard for Tammy. Hearing it sent Kathleen's emotions silently through the roof. It had never entered her mind that this was what she was going to hear.

"I want so much to make this a pleasant day for us both, so I had better get everything off my mind right away and then I can relax and be myself again. I

have one more thing to talk to you about, though,"
Tammy admitted. "Think about what I am going to
say before you make any decision. I'll understand."

"Just ask me, Tammy."

"Well, I had a long talk with Michael last night.
First, he asked me to tell you how grateful he is that
you are here. Then the bad news, his publisher
contacted him last night and told him it may be a
couple of more weeks on the road. They keep adding
cities that the publishers would like him to visit and
make presentations."

"You know I will stay," Kathleen said,
immediately. *Please God*, she said to herself, *let me be
strong enough to support Tammy now. It's not about me. It's
about her. It's about her dad.*

# CHAPTER 26

ⅮⅮuring the next few weeks, Kathleen did stay. There was no question in her mind. She was not leaving until Michael got back. She wanted to do whatever she could to help Tammy and there was a lot to tend to. Things like taking care of Tammy's lovely garden were easy.

There were social security records and information about his years in the navy to be located. Finding his insurance policies was what really took time. Eventually, Tammy found Kevin had the policies and naval records in a suitcase under the bed for some reason.

Tammy was pleased when Kathleen asked if it would be helpful if she addressed the envelopes for the thank you cards that were to be sent.

Kathleen wanted to help, but she was limited. "I can't do a lot of what is required, but I can do that."

"That would be great! You're right. I still have a lot of Dad's papers to look for. He wasn't great about keeping records, so I am going to have to do some searching. And by the way, thanks for the coffee break this morning. I needed it."

Around 2:00, they had a quick lunch and got back to work.

It was a cooler than usual day. Kathleen took the envelopes and the thank you lists out to the patio.

There was a flower list, a list of those that phoned or sent emails, and a list of those who dropped by with casseroles and desserts. Tammy had carefully recorded those who had been thoughtful.

A few hours later Tammy came outside and dropped in a chair. "I'm sure you know how much I appreciate your getting these envelopes done. That was another job I was dreading. Remind me tomorrow to get stamps."

Kathleen was busy. "Just a minute. I'm counting to see how many envelopes I've done. How many stamps we'll need. Sit back and rest for a few minutes. I know what it's like trying to gather all of the information. I had to take care of a lot of it when my mother died. They asked more questions than I thought necessary and some I didn't have answers for."

"I think I've completed the worst of it, thank heavens," Tammy sighed. "I'm physically and emotionally exhausted."

When the necessary information was gathered, Kevin's personal things were to be dealt with next. That was the hardest to do. Kathleen did all she could to support Tammy. One morning when they were sorting out Kevin's clothes to be given to Goodwill, Kathleen spotted the red shell lying on the top of a brandy snifter filled with shells. She walked over to the collection. *He had saved it all these years*, Kathleen thought as she picked it up and turned it over in her

hand. *It's ours! Those same three tiny white dots are still there!*
She gently returned the shell to the top of Kevin's shell
collection.

Gradually, Tammy and Kathleen got things in
some order and had a little time to sit back and talk.
Tammy wanted to tell Kathleen about her dad's life in
the navy. How he had risen to the rank of captain. She
told her of his many years commanding an aircraft
carrier, and finally, the heart attack that sent him
home.

Kathleen found comfort in learning the
missing pieces of his life.

IF…

## CHAPTER 27

One night with nothing good on TV, Tammy made a large pitcher of iced coffee and suggested that they go out on the patio and enjoy the breeze.

For a while they just sat back and tried to relax. Kathleen noticed, though, that Tammy seemed restless, unable to get comfortable and that was unusual.

Kathleen casually asked, "Anything on your mind, Tammy?"

Tammy jumped, spilling her ice coffee. "For heavens sake, what made you ask that?" *It was not like her to be so abrupt*, Kathleen thought, taken aback by her comment.

"I just wondered if there was something I could do to help."

"I'm sorry. I didn't mean to jump on you. There is something on my mind that I want to talk to you about and I just don't know how to start."

Kathleen was surprised. Tammy was always so sure of herself. Not knowing how to handle a situation didn't seem like her.

"We're not strangers, Tammy. Whatever it is, you might feel better if you get it off your chest."

Tammy knew she was right - but would Kathleen understand.

195

"Well, I'd like to tell you a little bit about why I loved my dad so much. We were so close. From the time I was a little girl, he told me stories of his life. About fishing and hunting with his father, helping his mom in the kitchen. He loved to cook. As I grew older he helped me with my homework, comforted me through my parent's divorce. The hardest part was when he had sea duty. I remember him explaining that this was his job. He said, 'make plans for my next trip home. We'll make up for lost time,' but gosh, it seemed forever. The waiting was so difficult."

Kathleen could see that Tammy was reliving those days as she talked.

Tammy went on. "We talked a lot during those last few days we had together. Among other things, he told me about a girl he had loved, still loves, and lost. How they were parted for what he thought would just be a short time and of how that wasn't the case. He said he had tried in every way he knew to find her. I couldn't understand why he was telling me this, but I listened. Then he spoke of the night he, Michael, and I had watched the *Noble* program on TV. Quietly he said to me, 'You must never give up hope, Tammy. You never know what is just around the corner.' Do you remember when I said that to you?"

Kathleen nodded. "I remember it well."

"And the last thing he said was, 'Tammy, I've found that girl that I loved, and still love. I had a dream of finding her for years, but I never expected to find her in my own home.' That made no sense to me and I asked him to explain what he was talking about. He said, 'It's Kathleen'." Tammy opened a small manila envelope that she had brought out on the patio with her. "I found this in one of Dad's file's." She pulled out a photo of Kathleen that had been taken on the first *Noble* cruise and handed it to her. "See the back also."

Kevin had written, *My Girl.*

There was total silence. Neither moved. Neither of them knew what to say. It went on for long time.

Not being able to hold back her emotions any longer, Kathleen suddenly jumped up and rushed back inside -- she had to get away. She ran up stairs and once in her room, she broke down. Her body racked as she lay on her bed, sobbing. Tears feel on the photo she held in her hand as she cried for Kevin, for the lost years. She cried for Tammy, too.

It was a long night for them both. They needed time. For Kathleen, it was a shock to learn that Kevin had confided to his daughter about her before he died. And even more of a shock was that Tammy had known about Kathleen weeks before Kathleen had arrived. Was Tammy happy to learn about her father and Kathleen? Kathleen wasn't sure.

Downstairs, Tammy was going through her own private hell. She spent long hours during the night wondering whether she should have told Kathleen of their conversation. Whether her dad would have wanted her to.

The next morning Kathleen showered quickly and dressed. She needed to get downstairs. She needed to see Tammy.

At the kitchen door she stopped abruptly. There was Tammy and a woman she didn't know, sitting on the floor playing with the dogs as they went roaring around the room.

Tammy heard Kathleen come in and looked up. "Get over here, Kathleen. I want you to meet my friend and the mother of these wild ones. This is Cathie Hendricks, my neighbor."

The woman quickly jumped up and grabbed Kathleen's hand. "Good morning, Kathleen. How nice it is to meet you. I'm so glad that you have been here with Tammy. She needed a friend to get her through these days."

Kathleen looked over at Tammy. They smiled at each other. Everything was okay. "It's good to meet you too, Cathie. I've fallen in love with these little ones of yours and I'm always available for dog sitting!"

Cathie laughed.

"Alright girls, enough talk. Let's have a cup of coffee and this luscious coffee cake that Cathie brought."

They had made it through the moment they had both dreaded. To herself, Kathleen said, *Thank you, Cathie.*

# CHAPTER 28

*I*n time, Tammy was notified by the navy about the final procedure for Kevin's burial at sea. It was his wish. For the past week, Tammy had worked on and completed all the forms.

Today, Kathleen helped Tammy prepare the urn for mailing to the navy. It was an emotional moment for both of them. Just before the box containing the urn was sealed, Tammy opened it. She pulled the red shell she had taken from the top of Kevin's collection from her pocket, and she placed it on his ashes. "Your memory is moving on with you, Dad," she said.

Kathleen had worried about how this hour would play itself out. She was cautious when she spoke to Tammy. "You've carried out all of your dad's wishes. There's nothing more to do."

"Yes, everything is as he had wanted and I'm so glad he'll be buried at sea. I'll wait for Michael to get home and ask him to take the box to the post office. He loved dad, too."

"Good," Kathleen said. "I'd like to stay here until Michael gets home and everything is taken care of."

"Of course, Kathleen, it's where I belong and where I want to be."

They wrapped their arms around each other for a full minute before Tammy's phone rang.

"That was Michael," Tammy told Kathleen. "He'll be in later tonight and asked that we don't hold dinner for him. Time's marching on, so let's find what we can throw together for dinner."

Kathleen and Tammy put together a little of everything that was in the refrigerator – mostly left overs from the day before. They continued talking about Kevin, Tammy's upbringing, and her productions. Two hours later Michael arrived by taxi.

When he walked into the living room where Kathleen and Tammy were having coffee, Tammy got up, kissed him, and asked, "How was that red-eye flight?"

"Not bad. Just long with everything you have to do at airports," he said, sounding very tired.

Michael walked over to Kathleen and gave her a big hug. "Glad you are safe and sound. Tammy has really been missing you."

"No more than I've missed her. I am so appreciative of your being able to spend so much time here with her. You're quite a friend, Kathleen."

"Thank you, but the time goes by too fast when I'm with wonderful people. We've had some important conversations, but now it's time for you two to spend time together. I think I'll take a little walk through that amazing garden of yours again before I go to bed." Kathleen turned to leave, but as she opened the door to the garden, she turned back to them. "Funny how things turn out, isn't it?" Tammy and Michael remained in the living room, talking and comforting each other.

Kathleen went out to the patio and walked through the garden. She needed quiet time – one last good-bye. She had been waiting to tell Kevin what was in her heart. She whispered as she walked along, "Our lives have taken us on so many turns, Kevin. After a while I thought we would never find each other." She hesitated and pulled a Kleenex out of her sleeve and wiped at her eyes. "I want you to know that I really tried, Kevin. Filling my days and nights wasn't easy. I tried moving on taking night courses, going with groups on tours, and even tried dating. Nothing worked. You and I learned in ten short days what love was all about. I have held it in my heart, Kevin - and you have, too. Tammy told me. I love you and I know it's not over. Our next trip is forever. Until then, you're off on your cruise."

Tammy took Kathleen to the airport early the next morning, so happy that Kevin's daughter would always be part of her life. As they drove, she felt peaceful, thinking, *all of the "if's" I wondered about for so long now had now been answered.*

Tammy's relationship with Kathleen did not end on that day that they said goodbye at the airport. They kept in touch. A few months later Kathleen had a call from Tammy. Her producer had notified her that a new show was in the works. Tammy said, "Here we go again Kathleen -- it may not be the

Caribbean this time -- it may be New England or Alaska. Who knows? The powers that be are just not going to let you fade from the scene - you were great the last time. We make a good team and they know it. Just keep your bag packed."

The program went on for three years. Kathleen and Tammy travelled worldwide, showing that age differences are a plus. Finally, back in Connecticut and with time on her hands, she and her sister renovated and sold their mother's house. Kathleen, with Mabel under her arm, downsized to condominium. Finally, she sat back and wrote her novel titled, *It's Never Over*. It was dedicated to Kevin Gordon Johnson, her friend for life -- and beyond.

**THE END**

IF...

TO YOU WHO MAKE MY LIFE MORE
WORTHWHILE THAN YOU WILL EVER KNOW.

## MY KIDS

WYNN AND DIANE AND CATHIE AND FRANK

## MY GRANDS

KATE AND MATT, WIN AND TIMARI, JOHN AND
JENNY, BEN AND SARAH, GEOFF AND CHELSEA,
AMANDA AND SCOTT

## MY GREATS

LEXI, LILY, ANTHONY, CAITLYN, LUKE, SIMON,
ZACH, GRIFFIN, JACK AND ABBY

# ABOUT THE AUTHOR

**Catherine K. Allen** is 93 years old. For 47 of those years, she was a travel consultant, traveling the world by air, sea, and land. She developed and coordinated travel plans for individuals, families, and corporations. Her specialty was creating personalized worldwide tours for clients – actually creating individualized vacations that would lead them through specific streets of a foreign city, offer critiques of delightful restaurants, and even preferable rooms in hotels allowing for the best views. Over the decades she published travel articles for "The Town Squire Magazine" (Kansas City), hosted the "Ask Kay" – a TV travel segment, presented travel seminars, taught travel in community college, and has completed a chapbook of her poetry. The American Society of Travel Agents (ASTA) presented her with the Crest Award for creative advertising utilizing verse. This is Catherine K. Allen's first novel, appropriately a travel-oriented romance story.